# KAT AND THE PENDULUM

# KAT AND THE PENDULUM

## Sam Stone

First Published in 2016 by
Telos Publishing,
5A Church Road, Shortlands, Bromley, Kent BR2 0HP,
United Kingdom.

www.telos.co.uk

Telos Publishing Ltd values feedback. Please e-mail us with any comments you may have about this book to: feedback@telos.co.uk

ISBN: 978-1-84583-948-2 (US Edition)



British Library Cataloguing in Publication Data. A catalogue record for this book is available from the British Library.

# DEDICATION

*For Sharna and Chace.*
It's been a tough year but I'm so glad you fought, and beat, cancer's arse! Don't scare me like that again please!

# ACKNOWLEDGEMENT

With thanks to Joshua Rainbird for originally suggesting
the title. This leant itself perfectly to another
Kat Lightfoot Mystery.

# Prologue

Bethany Precio threw back the covers and sat up in bed. Her body burned: the night heat was torture and she craved respite.

The castle was beautiful but oppressive. Yet everything about its design suggested it should be cooler inside, not hotter. Ever since she and Vincenzio had returned here from their honeymoon, she had struggled to sleep.

'My blood is boiling in my veins,' she had told him. 'Why do I suffer this damn heat so much?'

She turned her legs over the side of the bed and stepped to her feet.

Vincenzio was in the west wing. They had taken to sleeping separately since they had arrived here. She didn't quite understand why, but Vincenzio had said it would be nice for her to have her own set of rooms: her own space and privacy.

At first the idea had pleased her. She had never had so much space before. And the rooms had become a small haven, where she could take herself away to rest when the heat became too oppressive.

But then Vincenzio had become distant, as though by assigning her to her own rooms he had compartmentalised her. Often she found him sitting in the library alone, just staring at his desk. When she spoke to him he would look at her with no more than vague recognition. Bethany began to feel like she was merely something he had acquired. Not his wife at all, as he no longer wanted to spend time with her.

In the middle of the night those insecurities surged forward. Coupled with the cloying heat, they caused Bethany terrible pain.

*Everything hurts*, she thought. *This was meant to be our fairytale, and we would live happily ever after.*

Bethany opened the window, despite the fear of night-time parasites that might enter the room and bite her.

She looked out over the ramparts. Out over the oasis of vineyards.

What a beautiful home she had. Why couldn't she be happy?

Then came the awful screeching. Like a night owl caught in poacher's trap: its scream of fear was suddenly silenced as whatever had caught it broke its neck.

It was a noise Bethany had heard many times before. Vincenzio had said that it was nothing for her to fear or be concerned about – merely the movement of the castle at night – but Bethany experienced sheer terror every time that sound came. It was as though the place was haunted by an evil entity that tortured its victims when the occupants were all abed.

But for the heat, Bethany might have been able to sleep through this. But as she had become increasingly accustomed to the castle's creaks and groans, the brief shriek had begun to jar more and more with her, and now she woke just before it, like clockwork, every night.

She considered going to Vincenzio's rooms, but she remembered how it had turned out the last time she had gone to him for comfort. He had scorned her for her wild imagination and criticised her feminine weakness. She had returned to her own rooms feeling like a chastised child. The rejection from the man she loved had been just too much. She couldn't face that look of contempt again, and so she huddled by the open window, waiting for the next terrifying noise.

Unlike on other nights, the cold air did not cool her fevered body, nor calm her anxious mind. This time, the shrieks and wails went on and on, until finally Bethany was driven from her room.

Candle in hand, she planned to call on Vincenzio, beg him to be kind to her. She couldn't go on like this. The love she had thought she had for him was slowly dying, along with any self-esteem that she had.

Where had the man she had thought to be her best friend disappeared to? Why had he changed? They had enjoyed the most glorious honeymoon trip, but then this castle, his ancestral home, had brought about a terrible transformation in his behaviour. The sweet nature she had once thought him to have was replaced by that of a bitter and sneering tyrant.

She made her way down the corridor and to the landing, intent on waking Vincenzio, even if it did incur his ridicule; but at the top of the stairs she halted.

She glanced toward the west wing. Vincenzio should be in bed, but suddenly she had the feeling that he wasn't.

There was a creak under the stairs. She recognised the sound as the opening of the door that led down to the dungeons. She hadn't been down there, but knew her husband often did. It was another part of his life he had excluded her from.

Anger sent a hot flush into her cheeks. Why was he doing this? What manner of man would torment his wife, and shun her so soon after their honeymoon? What did she know about him anyway? Perhaps he had secrets; terrible secrets he wished to keep from her. If she could find out what they were, then maybe she could win back his trust in her ability to love him regardless.

Bethany began to walk down the staircase, but halfway down she faltered, almost losing her nerve. What would Vincenzio say if he caught her looking in the dungeon? She took a deep breath and continued down the steps. Somehow Vincenzio had already lost his respect for her, so what did it matter if he became angry with her too?

She reached the bottom of the stairs and turned toward the alcove beneath them. The normally-locked gate was open.

Bethany almost turned back, but the enticement was too hard to resist. There was something so inviting about the ornate wrought iron and the cherubic faces that smiled out at her from around the arched entrance.

She reached the gate before she was aware of walking forward, and even though her rational mind fought against her actions, some subliminal instinct overrode it.

*I have to see what is down there.*

Bethany passed under the arch as the gate opened wider before her. The flame of the candle in her hand wavered as a cool breeze wafted upwards.

Steps cut into stone led downwards.

For the first time, the feverish heat in her body was quelled. She revelled in the cool air and the cold stone beneath her bare feet.

There was music coming from below. The sounds of musicians playing at a ball. Bethany was propelled forward, and she began to descend the steps with no consideration of her informal attire.

A ball! A surprise ball! Vincenzio must have been

arranging this all along.

Her rational mind told her again that this was not right. Why would he do that in the middle of the night? But Bethany's subconscious stroked her anxiety away.

All was fine. Here was her destiny.

She reached the bottom of the steps and saw another doorway at the far end of a long corridor. It was cold down here. Bethany shivered, but not because the chill was unpleasant: there was something to fear, something she shouldn't and didn't want to see.

She couldn't stop herself, however, and she was hurrying forward as though her feet had a mind of their own. She thought of an old wives' tale of evil things taking over a person's soul. Of demons that could inhabit shoes, or clothing; that took control of your body. But Bethany's feet were bare, and the nightgown she wore was an old favourite. She knew that every step she took was because of her own subconscious desires.

The door ahead opened before her as though she was expected, and then Bethany entered the castle dungeon.

She looked down, and what she saw made her heart beat faster in her chest.

The dungeon branding pyre was alight. Its coals were glowing red hot, and a sulphurous smoke was ascending from the spikes and branding irons laid upon it. Her eyes moved over toward the wall, where a row of barred cells stood. There was coarse and matted hay within them, and as she looked, so she saw furtive movement as wretched inhabitants scuttled farther away from the heat of the torturers' implements. Horrible! Evil! Surely Vincenzio couldn't know of this?

The compulsion to see more finally left her, and Bethany turned back toward the door.

She found it closed and locked. Yet she hadn't heard

anything.

She was trapped. Trapped in a pit of despair. And down below, someone walked toward the steps wearing a black robe: looking for the entire world like those fearful inquisitors from her husband's ancestral past.

Her heart beat faster as she looked down and the robed spectre looked up.

Then Bethany screamed. It was the same sound she had heard every night since she had arrived there. The shrill, desperate call of an animal caught in a trap.

# 1

The air whistled past my ears as I leapt down from my vantage point on the fire escape above the street.

I landed without making a sound and followed the little girl as she walked confidently toward the bright gaslight ahead. She was wearing an expensive red coat. Her forelocks were pulled back and tied in a ribbon behind her head, while the rest of her fair hair cascaded down her back in rag-rolled curls. Of course, she wasn't really a little girl, she was some form of demon, otherwise she wouldn't have been out alone in the dark at two in the morning. And I wouldn't have been following her to see what she was up to.

There had been a spate of violent deaths in the last few days. A normal occurrence, you might think, in Manhattan; but the peculiarities of these murders indicated that they were not the work of gang members or petty thieves. No, these were unnatural in every sense.

My contact at the morgue had revealed some very odd details, and these had led me and my colleagues, Martin Crewe and George Pepper, to this street on this night.

The deaths appeared to be ritualistic: the heart was taken, as were the eyes of all of the victims; and the skin around the wounds was charred, as though the missing parts had been burnt out.

The girl turned off the main street now and headed down a very dark alleyway. No ordinary child would do that, for fear of attack.

I reached the entrance to the alleyway seconds before Pepper caught up with me. He'd had to climb down from his vantage point, because he lacked my skills and agility. But still, he was stealthy, and quiet.

Martin joined us a few moments later.

'What is it?' Martin asked.

'My best guess: some kind of demon possessing the girl,' I said. 'It's been taking the hearts and eyes of its victims. I'm thinking that this is somehow symbolic.'

'Could be just a cannibal,' Martin said. 'After all, they were cooked.'

'Nice thought,' said Pepper. He smiled at Martin's grim joke. In this job you had to keep your sense of humour or you would go insane.

I peered around the corner. The alleyway was full of dark shadows. Nothing moved. I could no longer see the little girl or her bright red coat. Yet I had the feeling that I was being watched.

'It's one of them and three of us,' I whispered. 'Let's go and see what she's up to.'

Martin placed his hand down on his gun belt. He was dressed, as my mother always said, like a 'gunslinger', with his stonewashed jeans, long lightweight coat and ornate cowboy shirt. On his hips hung the weapons belt, which held not only two high-powered guns, but also a knife and a pouch containing a lock-picking kit.

Beside him, Pepper had drawn his favourite gun: a laser flame-thrower that also had a regular bullet-firing mode, which was semi-automatic and could discharge over thirty shells in rapid succession. Pepper was wearing a conservative black jacket and a high-necked white shirt with a black tie. He also had on a tall black hat, which reminded me much of the style of Abraham Lincoln, our former President, who had been assassinated just the year before.

I was wearing my male breeches, a loose-fitting white shirt and a black jacket over it. I too wore a gun-belt, and on it I had a small pistol that Martin had devised to replace my much-loved, and now lost, Perkins-Armley purse pistol. My new weapon was again a Perkins, but it shot silver-tipped darts instead of bullets. We had learnt that silver was very toxic to demons, and that darts could penetrate the skin of the humans they possessed, driving them out. Sometimes, particularly in the case of short-term possessions, the victim survived. Martin was still working on improving the ratio in longer-term possessions.

My Perkins was the first weapon we would use on the child, in the hope that we could reclaim her body and soul and return her, relatively unscathed, back to her parents – whoever they might be. So I withdrew it now from its holster.

'I'll play victim …' I said, lowering my gun-arm to my side so that the creature wouldn't see I was armed.

The men nodded, so I turned down the alley and began to move as swiftly and quietly as possible into the gloom.

Once I was off the main street, shadows surrounded me – the gaslight barely touched this cavernous space. However, my eyes quickly adjusted to the dark – one of the many perks of my being a vampire/cat hybrid – and I could see fairly well. There were several trash cans clumped together near the back door of a closed restaurant. Rotting food spilled from the over-filled cans and cascaded down onto the ground. I heard the furtive scurry of rats amongst the trash. Then, as though they sensed me, a pack of the rodents burst from behind the cans and ran away in the opposite direction.

*That'll be the cat in me,* I thought.

My colleagues now entered the alley behind me. I was aware of them, but hoped the child demon wasn't. They had to rely on human vision, and I knew they would be unable to see as well as I could. To use their portable sunpan devices would make them too visible to the enemy, and we were hoping that we would be able to sneak up on her before she became aware of us, or else that she would see me alone and take me for a potential victim.

The alley was silent again after the rats had fled, as one might expect in the early hours before dawn. I reached the cluster of cans and paused.

My cat senses smelt something, or maybe it was the vampire side of me: blood.

I gave a low whistle, and grey tones and shapes flashed in front of my eyes. I had a rudimentary echo-location system that allowed me to see even better in the dark.

Eyes. Eyes everywhere. For a moment I almost wished that I not used my extra sense.

A dull thump and then another. The sounds of many beating hearts burst into play, and my vision opened up with more clarity. Yes. Here were the hearts. Here were the eyes. And all of them were working, just as though they were still attached to or a part of the people from whom they had been taken.

Pepper and Martin abandoned any attempt at stealth and hurried to my side.

'Good god!' said Pepper as he extracted his sunpan watch from his waistcoat pocket and raised it up above the trash cans.

The horror of it. I felt bile enter my mouth, and I swallowed it back. Then the smell hit me. Blood and rotting flesh. The hearts and eyes were somehow mounted onto the cans, and onto the wall behind: still beating or staring. My suspicion had been right: this was ritualistic in some way. The demon was using these still-living organs for something, and magic was controlling them.

There was no sign of the creature, however, and so I placed my dart gun back into its holster.

We stood there and studied the gory canvas, as the myriad eyes looked back at us.

A prickle of adrenaline made the hair stand up on the nape of my neck. I turned. The child was behind me. I could see her dark outline, and the flow of light from Pepper's watch spilt over her red coat. She had her head down, as though she was examining her shoes.

'Don't be afraid,' I said, hoping to reach the soul of the child, even if she was currently possessed. 'We are here to help.'

A burning pain took up in the back of my eyes and on the left side of my chest.

'I'm in need of you,' she said.

Her voice was cracked and old, and smoke poured from her mouth and nose. Even as she turned her head upwards to look at me, I knew that there was nothing of the child left inside.

A gash of a mouth leered at me, full of over-sharp teeth. The creature's eyes glowed red; burning coals in the centre of a hellish fire. The face was wizened, the nose hooked like that of the proverbial witch. But this was no witch. And no, this was not and never had been a child either. We had been seriously mistaken.

I knew what manner of creature it was, even though I had never seen one before. It was a Pyromaene – a demon that carried the fire of hell inside its own body. It burned with it.

Billowing smoke was wending its way across the alley toward me. I glanced at Pepper and Martin. They were both still looking the other way, seemingly transfixed by the sight of the heart and eye shrine; hypnotised, maybe, by the combined thudding of the beating hearts, which resembled the sound of tribal drums. I understood in that moment that this was how the creature captured her victims.

The heat increased in my eyes and chest: if I didn't run soon, my own eyes and heart would be added to this macabre display.

With an effort, I turned away from the Pyromaene. Then I grabbed my friends' arms and pulled with all of my strength.

They resisted for a moment, but my tugging was enough to help them fight the call of the heartbeat-drum, and once the spell was broken, they were moving of their own volition, running with me back down the alleyway the way we had come.

But the Pyromaene had not finished with us. With amazing speed and agility, it leapt into the air over our heads and landed in the alley before us, blocking our exit.

The creature breathed in, and its small frame began to expand.

'What's it doing?' I gasped.

'It's getting ready to strike,' Martin said.

'Strike?' said Pepper.

'Flame. Like a dragon,' Martin said.

The alley was sweltering hot, and I saw sweat drip down Martin's face. It was as though we had stepped from our own realm into the very embers of hell.

I gave Pepper and Martin a squeeze on their arms. We had our own signals, which we knew the creature wouldn't pick up. Both men nodded to show they understood what I was suggesting, then we all ran at once towards the creature, scattering at the last moment to divide its attention.

I pulled my Perkins dart-gun back out of my holster, and as I jumped over the creature in much the same way as it had somersaulted over us, I aimed the weapon downwards.

The creature tilted its head, its vile mouth impossibly wide, and I saw the pit of fire brewing inside its blackened throat. I shot down with the dart-gun; three darts flew into the demonic face. At the same time, Martin plunged his knife into the creature's chest. Then Pepper let go a round of silver-capped bullets into its back.

Hot smoke poured from the open mouth. I landed on my feet, turned and pointed my gun back at the thing.

Smoke poured from the wounds. Martin plunged the knife in and out repeatedly in a frenzied attack: aiming to injure the heart of the beast until it failed. Pepper meanwhile shot at its legs.

The thing's knee shattered and it tumbled to the floor. But still that open mouth puffed and expanded. Any moment, flame would pour from it, filling the alleyway. The thing might be dying, but it was determined to take us with it.

I ran forward, drawing its attention and, I hoped, all of its fire away from my friends. As the monstrous mouth expanded again, I shot my remaining darts into it.

The silver tips erupted and melted in the heat – but it

was enough. The Pyromaene flame was doused. The creature gagged and fell backwards, hook-clawed hands scraping at its disintegrating mouth and lips.

It was as though water had been poured onto hot coals. The thing sizzled, crackled. Sparks spat from its skin, igniting the nearby trash.

Flames burst over the cans. The hearts and eyes were soon consumed, and with them the final power that held the creature together was broken.

A ball of flame erupted upwards from its mouth. And then, the body set on fire.

Pepper ran around the flaming, flailing thing to join Martin and me on the other side.

We watched as the flames licked and burnt the red coat and the small child's shoes, while the blonde locks curled and shrivelled to nothing. It was grotesque and very difficult to watch.

'Horrible,' Pepper said. He was always the most sensitive to the horrors we saw, but this one would take a lot of eradicating from all our minds. Not least because of the childish guise it had assumed. That was the most horrible aspect of all.


Back at our headquarters, I threw aside my weapons-belt, and Pepper took off his coat and hat. Martin was wading through a pile of letters that he had collected from the post office earlier. We were all unusually quiet.

'Oh no!' Martin said suddenly.

Pepper and I turned to look at him. 'Bad news?' I asked.

'My sister is dead,' he said. His voice was flat with shock. 'I have to go to Spain.'

We hadn't even known he had a sister.

# 2

As the fifth day of our travelling drew to an end, we arrived, road dust weary, at the huge fortress of Vincenzio Precio. Our driver, Carlos, steered our carriage up to the huge double gates that were the only entrance, set into an otherwise perfectly secure wall that curved around, I assumed, the entire castle grounds.

The carriage came to a halt. I was inside with Martin and Pepper. We were here to pay our respects to the widower of Martin's sister, Bethany.

Martin had been quiet for most of the journey, first over sea and now over land, and Pepper and I had not pressed him too hard to share his emotions. It wasn't our way. We three worked together to cleanse the world of a very real and terrifying threat: the *Darkness* – the ultimate source of demon power – which was trying to work its insidious way into the world. We had fought it in many guises: demons, vampires, zombies – even the corruption of a Fae queen. You see, I am Kat Lightfoot, and I live a somewhat double life. During the daytime I am like any ordinary woman, but at night, with my friends, I am a demon slayer.

After the carriage stopped, Martin climbed out and

walked up to the gates. He tilted his head upwards. The gates were well over 30 feet tall – the same height as the wall – but in one of them there was a smaller doorway that was the obvious entrance for anyone arriving on foot.

I considered for a moment what Martin must be feeling, though his body language gave nothing away, as he reached for the long bell cord at the door and pulled.

I heard the bell inside ring loudly as, carriage sore, I too climbed out, eager to stretch my legs. Pepper limped out behind us. His leg had seized up from the long journey, and I knew that his old war wound would be giving him trouble.

It wasn't long before an aged servant answered the door and looked at Martin with a rather hostile expression. I was immediately curious about him.

'*Qué deseas?*' asked the man.

'*Quiero hablar con don Precio,*' replied Martin, who had shown a great deal of proficiency in the Spanish language – much to our surprise and delight, as this had made travelling through the country far easier.

'*Don Precio no está disponible,*' said the servant, making as though to close the door on us.

'He says, "Precio isn't available …"' Martin explained to Pepper and me.

'Wait!' I called out to the servant. 'We've been travelling for days.'

Martin introduced himself and explained that he was the former mistress's brother. This only made the servant even more nervous, and once again he attempted to close the door on us. It was curious behaviour indeed.

'What is all this commotion?' said a female voice from inside.

The servant turned and spoke in rapid Spanish, and then a petite and pretty young woman appeared, pushing the servant aside as she studied the three of us on the threshold. She had dark blonde hair and striking features, with intense blue eyes that made her look very different from anyone I would have expected to see in this region.

'I'm Martin Crewe.'

'Oh my goodness!' said the woman in perfect English. 'Of course! I remember you from the wedding. I'm Isobel Precio, Vincenzio's sister. Please do come inside. You all look weary.'

She then turned to the servant and spoke to him again in Spanish. He looked suitably chastised as he stepped back and allowed us to enter through the small door.

The large gates then opened, and our driver was directed to bring the carriage inside. Isobel gave the servant, whose name was Nicolas, instructions to lead the driver around to the stables and show him to the servants' quarters.

'Rest up for the next few days,' I told Carlos before he went. 'I'm sure we won't be here long.'

We walked through into a round courtyard, and Isobel led us toward the front of the fortress. This was not as impressive as the huge gates and high wall surrounding the keep. There was merely a single door, modest in appearance, leading into the castle itself.

'You must excuse Nicolas. Vincenzio rarely gets any visitors, and he was most peculiar even with me, when I arrived here last week.'

'You don't live here, then?' said Martin.

'Not permanently. I mostly spend my time in Madrid. But I received the letter telling me of … Bethany's illness and … passing. Vincenzio has been so upset, I had to come and spend a little time with him.'

'Perhaps you can help me,' Martin said. 'What did my sister die of?'

'Vincenzio will explain …' she said.

I exchanged a look with Pepper as Martin's further enquiries were rebuffed by Isobel, who would be drawn no more, other than to say she was very sorry for his loss.

'You'll all stay, of course,' said Isobel.

'Yes,' I said, without giving Martin a chance to reply for himself. 'Of course.'

I was very intrigued by this huge and gothic structure, and by the behaviour of Nicolas and Isobel.

Isobel led us into the main hallway then, and I was struck by the impressive staircase that curved upwards and round on the left side. Below was a large dining table, suitable for perhaps fifty or more people to be seated for a banquet. But the centrepiece of the room was a large fireplace, around which were arranged several comfortable chairs, a sofa and a small table. The fire was lit and blazing, and I soon realised that it was much needed: the thick castle walls permitted none of the intense Spanish heat to pass through from outside, and the immense reception room was gripped by a deathly chill that made me shudder as we entered.

'Please be seated,' said Isobel, and I perched on the edge of the sofa, near the fire. Pepper sat down beside me, but Martin remained standing, looking around the reception room.

Isobel pulled a bell cord by the fire and very soon another servant arrived.

'A jug of Madeira wine for our guests please, Mathias,' she said.

Mathias bowed and hurried away.

'You must forgive the slowness of service here, too,' Isobel said. 'This is a big castle and the kitchens are quite a distance from this room.'

Mathias returned with the Madeira and a tray full of

sweetmeats.

'An influence from the days of the marauding Moors,' Isobel said. 'But I rather like them.'

She picked up a small piece of pink paste from the tray and placed it in her mouth.

'Your English is excellent. In fact I'd swear you were English,' I observed.

'Vincenzio and I were educated in Cambridge,' she said. 'Our father sent us away to boarding school when we were both very young.'

'You must have missed your parents,' observed Pepper.

'Sadly, our mother died while we were both very small. I think our father didn't know what else to do with us. I suppose for him it was the best solution. And for us, it meant that we had no difficulty in fitting in with either Spanish or British aristocracy. Of course, Mr Crewe knows all of this already: Vincenzio met Bethany at the same boarding school. They were enamoured with each other almost right away.'

'I never heard the full story from Beth,' Martin said, 'but she was much younger than me, and after our father died, she went with Mother to live in England. Mother wanted to make a fresh start, so she got a job as governess at the school, which also meant that Beth was able to study there for free.'

'We were friends too,' said Isobel. 'I miss her.'

'Where is Vincenzio?' Martin asked. 'I'd really like to speak to him.'

'He's resting,' said Isobel. 'But I'm certain he will join us for dinner. We'll have that in the small dining-room, though.'

Nicolas reappeared then and spoke in whispered tones to Isobel.

'Your rooms are ready,' she said. 'Perhaps we should all go and freshen up, then meet down here at six o'clock for drinks before dinner? It will give you all a little time to rest after your journey.'

'Thank you,' I said. Road dust clung to my clothing, and the idea of changing and washing appealed a great deal.

# 3

Nicolas led us up the wide staircase. The banister was made from wrought iron, intricately woven with a design of black-faced cherubs. The stairs led up to a circular landing. At either side were two corridors: the castle had an east wing and a west wing. Nicolas turned and led us into the east wing.

'Where is Don Precio?' I asked the servant, on Martin's behalf. I knew he hadn't wanted to push too hard with Isobel, because of her polite and generous welcome.

'Resting,' Nicolas replied abruptly. 'He'll be down for dinner.'

I wasn't surprised to hear Nicolas's fairly good English, given that we now knew the Precio family had been educated in England.

'Your room,' Nicolas grunted to me. Then he handed me a key and walked away, leading Martin and Pepper back toward the west wing.

I found the door unlocked, and inside my trunk and carpetbag were already placed on the floor at the bottom of my bed: a four-poster with thick drapes hanging over the corners. The floors were made of polished and stained wood but scattered with a variety of rugs that looked expensive and exotic. A lit fire crackled in a hearth to one side. There was a dressing area beside an imposing wardrobe, which was screened off. Behind it I found a bathtub and a bureau with a bowl and jug for washing.

The Precio residence was obviously behind the times as far as bathroom facilities were concerned, but I didn't mind this light step back in history. It reminded me of all of the years we had been without our modern technology and gave me a sense of normality in my usually abnormal world.

I washed and changed, removing my travel skirt and jacket and slipping on a pair of breeches and a loose-fitting white blouse.

Now more comfortable in my regular male attire, I lay down on the bed, relaxing for a while. The journey had been very tiring, and the glass of Madeira, not to mention the heat from the fire, had warmed and relaxed me. I closed my eyes.

*I saw in my mind's eye a large clock and, inside, a pendulum that swung back and forth.*

I'm dreaming, *I thought,* of the passage of time.

*The swoosh of the pendulum grew louder, and I felt a breeze above my head as though I were now inside the clock base. I looked up and saw the pendulum swing; but then it was no longer a weighted ball but a sharp scimitar blade moving back and forth above my head.*

I heard a large *thunk* and opened my eyes. The room was in darkness, and for a moment I had forgotten where I was. Then the canopy over my bed began to make sense.

I heard the grinding of stone on stone. I froze. Then I

peered around the room through the slits of my eyes, without turning my head. If there was an intruder present, I didn't want them to know I was awake and aware of them.

One advantage I had was that the dark wasn't really an issue for me, given my echo-location abilities. But now there was no movement at all, and I could sense nothing.

A knock at the bedroom door brought me out of my semi-sleep. I had still been dreaming, I realised, and the sound I had heard must have been part of that.

'Kat?'

Instantly awake, I leapt from the bed and hurried to the door.

There was still a small amount of light coming from the fire as the last embers burned down in the hearth.

I opened the door and blinked at the burst of light from the candles in the corridor.

'I came up to fetch you. It's 6.15 …' said Pepper. He was looking very dapper in a smart smoking jacket, and was carrying a three-stemmed candelabra.

'Sorry! I fell asleep.'

'Are you coming down like that?' he asked, nodding to my breeches and shirt: it wasn't a judgement, just a question.

'I should probably change. Propriety and all that!' I said. 'Bring that light inside, will you?'

Pepper allowed me to lead him into my room, which was probably more of a decency *faux pas* than if I had gone to dinner in men's clothing. But he was used to being around me in various states of undress, and he handled this latest indiscretion with barely a raised eyebrow.

I pulled a dress from my trunk, shook it out and then glanced at Pepper. He was doing a very good job of examining his fingernails as I pulled off the white blouse and tossed it over onto the bed. I was in my breeches with a short chemise tucked into them. I untucked the undershift and then pulled the dress over my head, leaving the breeches underneath. It was a red velvet evening dress, which fastened at the back.

'Help me with this thing, will you?' I asked.

Pepper dutifully placed the candelabra on the cabinet beside the bed and then, with the skill of a long-suffering husband, ran the laces through the corseted bodice and pulled me in tight as I held onto the bedpost.

'You're getting rather good at that,' I observed.

'I've had a lot of practice,' he said.

I laughed. It was true that Pepper helped me in and out of clothing all the time when we were on our adventures. One moment we could be at a ball, the next I'd need to rip away my gown as we chased down some evil being. After we had caught and disposed of said creature, he would then have to help me look presentable again.

'It really is a bind sometimes – having a double life,' I said. 'Especially with this awful corsetry.'

'Well, tonight you get to be a lady instead of a demon-slayer. Perhaps a little break will be good for us all.'

'Mmm.'

Pepper tied my laces, then picked up the candelabra and walked to the door, just as it opened inwards.

We came face to face with a tall, imposing man wearing a blue velvet smoking jacket with a cream cravat loosely tied around his neck. He carried a candelabra similar to the one that Pepper had brought.

'You have been invited to dinner,' he said in brusque but perfect English. 'Kindly be on time.'

'I'm sorry,' I said. 'I needed a little help, and I forgot to ask *Doña* Isobel if there was a maid who ...'

He looked me up and down as though I were a common street girl who had dared to talk to him.

'I am Vincenzio Precio, and it is hardly fitting …' said Vincenzio.

'We're married,' Pepper said quickly, realising that Vincenzio's old-fashioned values meant he was judging me wrongly. 'Very recently.'

'My brother-in-law, Martin, referred to her as *Miss* Lightfoot,' Vincenzio said.

'On the ship. Crossing to Europe,' Pepper said. 'We didn't have time to explain to Martin.'

'Nor buy a ring?' sniffed Vincenzio.

'Oh, we have a ring,' said Pepper.

Then, much to my surprise, he retrieved a small box from his jacket pocket.

'Here, darling,' he said. 'I brought it from my trunk as I promised.' He turned to Vincenzio again, and explained: 'It was a rather expensive ring, and Katherine was worried about wearing it as we travelled.'

I couldn't have looked more taken aback if I had tried.

I took the box, opened it and gazed down at my former engagement ring. Pepper had given it to me when during an earlier adventure, when we had both been under the influence of a vampire's spell. When the evil enchantment had been beaten, I had returned the ring to him, expecting him to take it back to the shop he had purchased it from. I had never expected that he would hold onto it. Nor that he would have it on his person so conveniently.

I took the ring out of the box now and dutifully slipped it onto my finger, playing the role so easily that Vincenzio had no reason to doubt us.

'Thank you for taking care of it … darling,' I told Pepper, and he slipped his arm casually about my waist and placed a kiss on my forehead.

Vincenzio, seeing that the ring fitted my finger perfectly, immediately changed his attitude.

'My goodness! If we had known we had newlyweds then Nicolas would have given you a room together!'

'That's fine,' Pepper said. 'It's so new to us both that it didn't occur to us either.'

'We'll have that rectified while we are at dinner,' Vincenzio said. 'This is the bigger room, so I'll have Nicolas move your things in here, Mr …?'

'Pepper. George Pepper,' Pepper said, holding out his hand for the formal introduction.

'And you are now Mrs Pepper, then, and not Miss Lightfoot,' Vincenzio enthused. 'How pleased I am. Why, this news brightens up our dull quarters.'

'Oh, please … ' I said. 'Everyone just calls me Kat.'

'*Doña* Kat then,' Vincenzio said. 'If you are ready, I will lead you both to the dining-room.'

'Of course,' said Pepper taking my arm.

# 4

'Congratulations are in order!' Vincenzio said.

We sat down at a grand table in the dining-room as Vincenzio raised his glass to us. I had been placed next to Pepper, opposite Martin and Isobel.

Vincenzio was at one end of the table, and at the other, a place had been set, but no-one occupied it. It was as though Vincenzio was waiting for Bethany Precio to appear for dinner, weeks after she had died.

'Why congratulations?' asked Martin after Vincenzio gave his toast.

'Your friends' marriage. On their journey here. You must be so pleased for them.'

Martin's eyes narrowed, and I gave him a very quick look that said, *I'll explain later.*

'Oh yes! Of course. They were waiting for the right moment,' Martin said quickly.

'How romantic to be married on board a ship,' Isobel said.

Pepper took my hand. 'We thought so.'

Martin said nothing, but a half smile touched his lips.

The servant Nicolas came around the table with a wine decanter and filled our glasses. When it seemed acceptable, I withdrew my hand from Pepper's and picked up my wine glass. I sipped some of the full-bodied wine as a way to distract myself from the embarrassment of our current misunderstanding. Why couldn't society accept that a man and a woman could just be best friends, as Martin and Pepper were to me? It was a source of frustration that I had to justify our relationships all the time.

'Did you have a long engagement?' asked Isobel.

'Mmm.' I swigged from my glass again. 'Excellent vintage, *Don* Vincenzio.'

'It is made with grapes from our own vineyards,' Vincenzio said. He was pleased that I liked it. 'Our family has made wine of this quality for centuries.'

'I believe we passed through the vineyards on our journey here,' said Martin. 'I wondered if they belonged to you.'

Nicolas placed a bowl before me. It contained lumps of bread and bits of garlic floating in a thin soup. After everyone had been served and our host had begun to eat, I tasted the soup and was surprised to find it cold.

'It is gazpacho,' Isobel explained. 'An ancient recipe brought to Spain by the Romans. But it is now a local delicacy that I thought you might appreciate.'

I ate out of politeness but wasn't sure I liked it. Fortunately, the next course that came was a more familiar one of roast beef and potatoes – in keeping with our hosts' Britishness.

After dinner, we all gathered once more in the large reception room. Now that I wasn't so tired, I noticed the two attractive tapestries that hung from the walls. One was of an ancient Greek parable that I didn't recognise but the other depicted images of the Spanish Inquisition. A row of men representing Jews and Muslims were expelled from the country. Some of the images showed men and women of these faiths kneeling before an altar as they were forced to pledge allegiance to Christianity. The tapestry was hand-woven, and was certainly beautiful and well made. However, I could not help but feel that the content was less than wholly appropriate for a formal reception room.

'I see you looking at the tapestry,' Vincenzio said. 'My father commissioned it. For almost 400 years the Inquisition was part of our Spanish heritage.'

'Thankfully abolished in 1834,' Isobel said. 'Vincenzio and I have little tolerance for bigotry.'

'I keep the tapestry as a reminder,' said Vincenzio, 'of a time when many wrongs were done to many innocent people.'

'Quite so,' said Martin. 'And now that dinner is over, you'll forgive me for asking, but I must know.: please tell me what happened to Bethany. Your note was so vague.'

'Please, Mr Crewe,' Isobel said. 'Could we not discuss this tomorrow? Let us not ruin such a lovely evening and the celebration of your friends' marriage.'

'That's okay,' I said. 'We came here to support Martin, and I'm sure he'll sleep better tonight knowing the truth.'

Vincenzio's face became a mask of torture. 'This is truly difficult for me. You must know that I loved my wife … *You* have a look of Beth, my dear. It is truly remarkable. It was why I was so shocked when I first laid eyes on you.'

'Me?' I said.

'Vincenzio is right,' Isobel said. 'I saw it in you immediately.' She stood and went to her brother's side, then placed her hand on his arm. 'This is so distressing for him. Should I explain for you, brother?'

Vincenzio appeared to be choking back tears of grief.

He nodded to Isobel, then turned away from us to compose himself. He stared down into the fire, as though he was seeing the past few months dancing in the flames.

'My brother loved Beth. They were barely ever apart. And after their honeymoon he was thrilled to bring her back here to our family estate. I was here when they arrived, but when Beth had settled in, I returned to Madrid to pick up the pieces of my own social life. They both promised to come and visit but, unfortunately, that wasn't to be.'

Martin was now staring into the fire like Vincenzio. His face was unreadable, but I knew that blank mask better than most. He was hurting, and it was all he could do to stop himself from demanding an answer. 'What happened?' asked Pepper, on his friend's behalf.

'Bethany developed a fever,' Isobel replied. 'Probably brought to her through an insect bite. Slowly she slipped away, and despite the help of our family doctor, nothing could be done.'

'A fever? Malaria perhaps?' said Martin.

I didn't need any reminder of how intelligent Martin was. But our hosts glanced at each other for a second, and then Isobel returned her attention to him once more.

'Why, yes. I believe it was. Something of that nature; at least, the doctor believed it was.'

'Strange. Malaria is carried by mosquitoes. But usually only in tropical and subtropical climes. I have not known it to be common in Spain. Could your doctor explain how Bethany contracted such an illness?'

Isobel didn't answer; she glanced at Vincenzio, but he remained still, as though in some kind of awful trance.

'Well … I don't know,' said Isobel finally. 'I wasn't here.'

'*Don* Vincenzio,' I said, 'could the doctor have been

wrong about her illness?'

'We travelled on our honeymoon,' he said slowly, 'passing through India, where such diseases do exist. I recommended doses of quinine, but Bethany wouldn't take it. She said she couldn't stomach it. It was two weeks after we returned here that she began to show the symptoms. Fatigue, fever, sickness and head pain. I sent for our family doctor and he diagnosed her illness. Soon afterwards, she fell into a coma. After that, she merely slipped away.'

Martin put his head in his hands for a moment. Then he looked up. 'Wait. You said this was just a few weeks after you came home from your trip?'

'Yes,' Vincenzio nodded.

'But that was months ago! Beth has been dead for months, and yet you wrote to tell me only recently.'

'He was in mourning,' Isobel said. 'He didn't tell me until recently either. You must understand, Vincenzio is devastated by Bethany's loss.'

'Of course he is,' I said, as I felt the tension rising in the air. 'But obviously this is also very hard for Martin.'

Isobel nodded. 'I know. I'm sorry.'

'We're all tired. And this has come as a shock,' Pepper said. 'Perhaps we ought to sleep on it and discuss it again in the morning.'

He placed his hand on Martin's shoulder and squeezed, giving him one of our warning signals. I knew then that, like me, Pepper was greatly suspicious about the sudden death of Bethany Precio. And if I knew Martin at all, then he too would be making complex calculations in his head that disproved everything that Vincenzio had said about his sister.

'Very well,' said Martin. He stood then, and after bowing over Isobel's hand, wished her and Vincenzio a good night.

Pepper and I soon followed, and when he walked me back to my room, we found Nicolas waiting for us.

'All your cases are now in with the *Doña's*,' Nicolas told Pepper.

'Oh. Right,' said Pepper.

Nicolas handed Pepper the key to the room, and both of us entered, closing the door on the grinning servant.

'Well, that wasn't awkward at all,' I said.

'Sorry. I had to think quickly I didn't want Vincenzio to judge you badly.'

'Interesting, isn't it, that in this so-called advanced world, where science is making extraordinary progress, I would be the one with the bad reputation and you would not be frowned upon at all.'

'I do agree. You know that. It isn't right or fair.'

'Well, this room's a lot bigger than the cabin we shared on the ship, so I don't think it will be too much of a problem,' I said.

'Unlike in the cabin, there is no couch. But the bed is big enough. I can put some cushions between us if it makes you feel better?'

'Pepper, we are friends. I've slept in the same bed as girlfriends before. Why should this be any different?' I slapped his shoulder in a particular man-friend way. 'Help me out of this dreaded thing, will you?'

Pepper began to unfasten the laces of the dress, and once it was loose I stepped behind the screen with my nightshift and robe and stripped it away. Then I tossed the dress and my breeches onto a chair and came out, tying my robe. Pepper was already in the bed, wearing his long johns. I pretended not to notice as I slipped into the other side and pulled the covers up over me.

'Night Kat,' he said, blowing out the candles, which

were on his side.

'Night Pepper,' I said, and that was when all hell broke loose.

# 5

There was a tremendous screech, like metal grinding on metal. I jumped out of the bed, pulled off my nightgown and tugged my breeches back on over my hips. At the same time, Pepper was also dragging on the clothing he'd discarded. He lit the candles by the bed just as I dropped the white shirt over my head. I tucked it in and opened my carpetbag, retrieving a small, pre-loaded pistol, which I pushed into my waistband.

The noise continued to echo through the castle. Like fingernails scraped across a child's writing slate.

Pepper was at the door, with the candelabra in one hand and his pistol in the other. Neither of us had time to load a more efficient weapon, such as my semi-automatic Remington: the backpack containing the bullet cartridges was in my trunk, but there was no time to retrieve it, strap it on and connect it to the gun. These more conventional weapons would have to do for now.

Pepper opened the door, and the screeching sound grew louder … to ear-piercing levels. I could tell now that it was coming from below us.

'What *is* that?' I whispered.

'It sounds like a stuck pig,' said Pepper. 'But I'm pretty

certain it isn't.'

We hurried toward the staircase and the source of that awful noise.

Martin was already on the landing looking down into the vast hallway.

'Where's it coming from?' Pepper asked.

'The dungeon,' Isobel said, emerging from her room. She was rubbing her eyes.

'Dungeon?' I said.

'It will be Vincenzio. He is maintaining the machinery.'

Martin and I exchanged a glance.

'What machinery?' asked Martin.

'Take us down there,' Pepper said.

Isobel looked shocked. 'Down? There? I never go down to the dungeon.'

The shrieking noise of this so-called machinery abruptly stopped.

'There, it's finished,' said Isobel. 'It never goes on for long. We all just need to go back to bed and get some rest.'

'Not until I see this machinery,' I said as I began to descend the staircase.

Martin and Pepper followed.

'Wait!' called Isobel. 'You can't. We aren't permitted …'

'Blame us for not knowing that,' said Martin. 'But we are going into that dungeon. And now.'

As we reached the bottom of the stairs, Vincenzio came into the hallway from a door under the staircase. I hadn't noticed it earlier, because it was hidden under an ornate wrought-iron arch. The iron gate beyond matched the balustrade of the staircase, and grinning cherubs decorated it.

'Can I help you?' he asked. He pulled the gate closed behind him.

His fingers were stained with black grease and he was

wiping them on an old rag. I had seen such machine fat before, on Martin's hands when he was maintaining our weaponry or oiling some piece of gadgetry. Often it was used on the engine of his airship. I couldn't help but wonder what kind of mechanism Vincenzio might have that needed to be oiled, and why it would be so noisy when used.

'What was that noise?' asked Pepper.

'Nothing to trouble you,' said Vincenzio. 'An old mechanism installed by my father. I need to maintain it sometimes.'

'May we see it?' I asked.

'Such things are not for women's eyes,' Vincenzio said.

Fortunately he appeared too tired to notice my male attire, or doubtless he would have frowned upon that too. Vincenzio passed me and began to climb the stairs, which was just as well for him, because I was about to give him a piece of my mind. He appeared to be in some kind of trance, though he did glance at Isobel as she waited halfway up the stairs. Again there was that anomalous unspoken exchange between them, before Vincenzio turned and walked away, toward the east wing and his bedroom.

'*Doña* Isobel,' said Martin, 'I think you need to come down here and show us this dungeon, and the mechanism that your brother was "maintaining".'

Isobel shook her head. She was afraid, and of what, we had to find out.

'I can't,' she said. 'It's not permitted. You heard my brother. Women aren't allowed in the dungeon.'

'Why?' I asked.

'I don't know,' she said. 'We just aren't. It was a rule our father set, and Vincenzio has kept it ever since he took over the maintenance.'

Martin walked to the door under the stairs and tried to open it. 'It's locked.'

'Of course it is,' said Isobel. 'It's *always* locked.'

'Are you telling me you've *never* been down there?' I asked.

'It isn't permitted.'

Then Isobel turned and hurried back to her room.

'I can pick the lock,' said Martin, as Pepper and I joined him under the staircase.

'It would be rude,' I said. 'Let's sleep on it and maybe speak to Vincenzio again tomorrow. Perhaps he'll give you men a tour, and you won't have to resort to deceit.'

'All right,' said Martin. 'Now, what was all that wedding stuff about? You didn't really get married on the ship, did you?'

'Of course not,' I laughed. 'We were caught in an awkward situation earlier.'

I explained Vincenzio's rather blinkered attitude and our plight now of having, once more, to pretend we were married.

'I couldn't have him judge Kat like that,' Pepper said.

'You did the right thing. I'm still a little uncomfortable that both of them think Kat looks like Beth.'

'Does she?' Pepper asked.

'I hadn't thought of it. She has the same colouring. Dark hair, blue eyes. But, well, the truth is, I hadn't seen that much of my sister over the years, and I didn't make it to the wedding.'

'But … Isobel said you two met at the wedding,' I pointed out.

'I didn't want to correct her. She probably confused me with someone else.'

The three of us climbed the staircase and parted once more at the top, as Pepper and I went west and Martin east.

Back in our room, Pepper placed the candlestick down by the bed.

'What do you make of all of this?' I said.

Pepper shrugged. 'It's hard to switch off our natural suspicion, isn't it? I mean, it's more likely that Bethany Precio did contract malaria on her honeymoon and died through completely unfortunate, but non-supernatural, circumstances.'

'I'm hoping that's the case. It would be a change,' I said. 'But Isobel's brother is a chauvinist.'

'It looks that way. We're all tired. The man lost his wife. I guess we should give him a little leeway. I'll talk to him tomorrow, and we'll definitely get down into that dungeon and make sure nothing untoward is happening.'

'You think something unsavoury is happening down there?'

'No. I think tomorrow will prove that the man is just a little eccentric.'

'Okay. But I'm telling you now, my cat senses are twitching. Despite what I said to Martin, I want to get down there. Perhaps you and I could take a look without him? After all, Beth was his sister. I'd hate to upset him. But if we find anything, we can call him in then.'

'What do you think we will find down there?'

'I don't know. But something isn't right about this place.'

Pepper sat down on the edge of the bed. He was thoughtful.

'All right. But let's give everyone else a chance to get to sleep before we go snooping.'

# 6

All tiredness fled once Pepper agreed to go exploring the dungeon of the Precio castle with me. If nothing else, it was an adventure, whatever we found. I opened my trunk and rummaged inside until I found my sunpan torch, which was disguised as an ornate bracelet. I placed it on my wrist. Pepper had a similar light in the form of a pocket watch, which he now attached to his smoking jacket. Independent of candles, we would have light to guide us, and could switch it off at any time if we were in danger of being observed.

Pepper also found his lock-picking kit, which he placed in his pocket.

Once armed, tooled and ready, we sat side by side on the bed, waiting for complete silence to fall in the castle. Since becoming half cat/half vampire[1], I had gained profoundly acute hearing, so I could pick up all the movements of the household and tell when varying degrees of stillness came over the castle.

'The servants are down for the night,' I said. 'We can make a move now.'

---

[1] See *What's Dead PussyKat.*

I went to the door, opening it as silently as possible. Pepper blew out the candles.

Outside, he locked the door, then placed the key inside his jacket pocket. With the door locked it was unlikely that anyone would find out that we had left the room, unless they were determined to do so. My suspicious mind already believed that something was very wrong about this place; I just didn't know what it was yet.

Proceeding stealthily was something we were good at. Pepper moved ahead of me; and it was at these moments that I could no longer make out his limp. We descended the stairs, and because these were made completely of stone, there wasn't even a creak to give us away.

We reached the bottom and turned toward the arch underneath and the door that led down to the dungeon. I stood at the arch and looked out onto the hallway, keeping my ears and eyes open for any sign of the servants coming, while Pepper picked the lock.

'Kat,' he whispered.

I went to him.

'It's already unlocked,' he said.

'Martin?' I said.

'Let's see.'

The iron door opened with a barely perceptible creak. I glanced up at the hinges and noted they were smeared with grease.

'Martin for sure,' I said.

Pepper glanced at the hinges and nodded. Who else would think to grease the hinges to cover any noise they might make?

Pepper passed through the doorway and I pulled it shut behind us so that the casual glance wouldn't notice it was disturbed.

I followed Pepper down the narrow and somewhat

claustrophobic corridor and we came to a flight of steps that led downwards. I switched on my bracelet for Pepper's sake. I didn't need it, because I could have used my echo location-ability. Even so, it was probably advisable that we didn't make any noise at all until we had seen into this mysterious dungeon.

The steps were of stone. They appeared to have been cut into one solid piece of rock, and they led down into a pit of blackness. Many times before I'd found myself wandering about in dark cellars, and now it seemed I was going to have a dungeon to add to those experiences. There were always dark places to investigate wherever we went, and I couldn't help reflecting on that detail now. However, the darker it grew, the stronger the glow from my newly-revised bracelet became. Martin had made sure that this technology was capable of assessing the degree of darkness and reacting to it accordingly. The light spilt ahead of my outstretched arm and filled the void in front of us. Consequently we were able to see the end of the steps, and an arched opening out of the narrow staircase.

At the end of a small antechamber, there was a large oak door. It was slightly ajar, and a glow of light came from the room beyond.

I turned off the bracelet light as we reached the final step and Pepper and I edged forward toward the door. On the other side we could see more steps leading downwards into a wide dungeon area. We stopped by the door and peered through the gap. There were several torches burning, and the space was well lit. Along one side there was a row of cells, which looked empty and abandoned. Other than some manacles strung from the walls, as though left there for dramatic effect, the dungeon was completely empty.

I was surprised, and I glanced at Pepper to see his

reaction also.

'Nothing there ...' he whispered.

'True. But why is it lit up?'

'Martin taking a proper look, perhaps?'

I wasn't convinced, but I put my hand on the door and pushed, causing it to swing open with a gentle creak of aged wood and protesting hinges. Beyond was a flight of perhaps 15 more stone steps.

'It's a former torture chamber,' said Isobel.

Pepper and I jumped with surprise.

Isobel had been standing in shadow inside one of the cells. As she spoke, she walked forward so that we could see her. The light from the flaming torches was playing across her face.

'What are you doing here?' I asked.

'Maybe I was curious. Like you.'

I walked down the steps, wary of the open side that plunged down onto the hard floor below.

'You've *never* been down here?' I said.

Isobel didn't answer.

'Quite a place ...' said Pepper. 'Bet there's some awful history here.'

'There is,' said Isobel. 'You see, our father worked for the Inquisition. Vincenzio told me that he did terrible things down here.'

'What kind of things?' I asked.

'Torture. Murder. Probably worse than that ...'

'That isn't a very nice history to have,' said Pepper. 'Quite a burden for anyone to carry.'

Isobel smiled. 'Of course I made all that up. Nothing happened here at all, except for a few social gatherings ...'

'I beg your pardon?' I said.

'Sorry. I'm not good at building a sinister story. I always laugh and give the game away. Vincenzio is far better than me. This used to be a storage area for the castle. My mother had it turned into a fun place to bring guests when they had one of their many parties …' Isobel laughed. 'After she died, father no longer had the heart to use it. So Vincenzio made up this whole scenario for fun.'

'What scenario?' asked Pepper.

'That this was once a *real* torture chamber. That Mother died down here, by our father's hand. None of it is true. It is just a story he likes to tell visitors. But first he makes out that women aren't permitted, so that we all want to come down here and look. He teased Beth with it when he brought her here. Eventually, when he did show her and told her it was a joke, we all had a good laugh about it.'

Her laughter pealed around the room, and I wondered if it was enough noise to wake Martin and Vincenzio. It set my teeth on edge.

'What a strange sense of humour you and your brother have,' I said.

'Yes. But you'll see the funny side when he does the whole drama tomorrow. You *must* go along with it, though. He's rather good. He was always doing plays at our school in England.'

'I think we ought to retire,' Pepper said, taking my hand.

'Good night, Isobel,' I said, and both Pepper and I turned back up the stairs and walked away.

I generally have a good sense of humour, but I didn't really see the funny side of Vincenzio's planned little game with us, particularly in light of Martin's sister's death. It was more than a little tasteless.

Back upstairs we made sure our bedroom door was locked and repeated our earlier ritual of changing. Then we went back to bed without saying another word.

# 7

Breakfast was a solemn affair, with Vincenzio sitting sullenly at one end of the table and Isobel smiling slyly at us from across the other side. It was as though they had totally forgotten everything that had happened the previous night; but Pepper and I, although we hadn't discussed it, were still digesting the information we had gathered from Isobel.

'I'd like a tour of your dungeon,' Martin said. 'But I insist that Kat and Isobel be permitted to come too.'

Vincenzio looked up from his breakfast, and an odd gleam was in his eye. If I hadn't known of his deception, I would have considered it a mark of insanity. Oh, but he played it well. Just as Isobel had said he would.

'Very well,' he said. 'We'll go downstairs after breakfast. But maybe the ladies should eat lightly, lest the horrors below should sicken them.'

'I have a strong stomach,' I said.

I didn't look over at Isobel.

Soon after, we retraced our steps of the previous night, this time with Vincenzio as our guide. Isobel was hanging onto Martin's arm, which was odd for me to see, since I hadn't noticed him giving her that much attention the previous night. Now he appeared to be concerned about her welfare, and he treated her like some fragile flower that might swoon at any time.

Isobel looked petite and slender, but appearances are often deceptive. I had already realised she was not that sort at all.

'*Kat!*' whispered Pepper. 'Your teeth ...'

I realised I was grimacing and showing a little fang, so I closed my mouth and smiled a thank you to Pepper, who always looked out for me. I needed to retain my focus: what was wrong with me?

Vincenzio unlocked the door – which Isobel must have resealed the night before – and it opened silently on greased hinges. Vincenzio didn't comment on the lack of sound though. He led us down the narrow stone steps and into the dungeon.

When he swung open the wooden door leading into the dungeon, Pepper and I exchanged glances. The room had changed overnight. No longer was it bare. Now it was filled with devices of torture. A rack to stretch victims on and pop their joints; an iron maiden standing ajar, the interior studded with spikes; a brazier burning fiercely with a branding iron thrust inside.

Then I noticed that the cells were now occupied.

A man sat on filthy hay in the corner of the first cell, wearing a bright court jester's costume that was ripped and stained as though he had been imprisoned for many months. In the next cell, a woman hung from manacles on the wall. Her hair was matted and filthy, and her milkmaid's clothing was torn from her back as though she had been whipped. The third cell held a little street urchin. His sat with his hands through the bars, arms outstretched as though pleading for his life.

'What is this?' demanded Martin.

'The Precio dungeon,' Vincenzio said. 'Where all manner of torture and abuse took place ...'

And then he began to tell us the tale that Isobel had said he would, about how his father had worked as the chief interrogator for the Inquisition.

I looked over at Isobel while Vincenzio spoke, and she was obviously enjoying this crazed and bloody story. Martin put his arm around her shoulders as though he wanted to protect her from this horror. But Vincenzio was oblivious as he acted out his part as a terrifying narrator. He gloried in the gore of the tale.

Then, when he got to the part about his father murdering his mother for being faithless, his tune suddenly changed. He spoke with less drama, as though he were merely reciting words that someone had scripted for him, and that had no meaning for him.

Isobel began to laugh. 'Oh brother, dear, you are so hilarious!'

Vincenzio stopped talking and then smiled. 'But of course this is all utter nonsense!'

As Vincenzio and Isobel explained their little joke, I realised then that the figures we had seen in the cells, although lifelike, did not move at all, and were in fact waxwork carvings.

'Excellent workmanship,' I said, examining the hands of the little boy. 'He appears real!'

'An amazing legacy created some twenty years hence by Marie Tussaud,' explained Vincenzio. 'My parents commissioned them when they visited England and saw her museum in Baker Street. They had great fun creating this dungeon for their friends' amusement.'

'*Don* Vincenzio,' said Martin, 'I'm almost at a loss for words. We are here because of my sister's tragic death. Last night you seemed distraught, barely able to speak of it, yet today you are … performing some theatre for our amusement! I want to see my sister's grave, and I want to speak to the doctor who treated her!'

With that, Martin turned away and walked back upstairs out of the dungeon. Pepper and I followed.

I should have realised that Vincenzio's joke would backfire, yet I had been so taken in by it myself that I had scarcely considered Martin's feelings. Pepper took my hand and squeezed it as we reached the reception hallway. I looked at him, and his normal ready smile had given way to a grimace. We had been incredibly insensitive in not taking Martin's reaction into account.

'Sorry,' Pepper said to Martin as we caught up with him.

'What is going on here?' Martin asked. 'I feel as though we have just walked onto a stage, set for our amusement.'

'Technically, that is what just happened down there,' I said.

'Not the actions of a grieving widower,' Martin said.

I wanted to agree with him, but didn't voice my thoughts, because Isobel had come up from the dungeon and was approaching Martin.

'I apologise,' she said. 'Vincenzio's humour has suffered since Beth's death. I admit that I encouraged him to act out our favourite game. I didn't think about how it would affect you.'

Martin permitted her to hug him, though he stood rigid in her arms.

'Come, I'll take you to the graveside now,' she went on. 'Normally family members are interred in a crypt below the dungeon room. But Beth left a wish that she be buried near the vineyards.'

The three of us followed Isobel out of the castle and into the courtyard. Waiting, as though pre-prepared, was

Nicolas perched in the driver's seat of a horse-drawn buggy big enough to carry the four of us. Martin helped Isobel into the buggy first, and Pepper and I climbed in and sat opposite her. Martin was last in, and he took the seat beside Isobel.

Isobel didn't give Nicolas any instructions, but once we were all seated, he set the horse off toward the gates, which opened up as we reached them. We passed through and headed out into the already blazing sun toward the vineyards.

A few miles away from the castle, a small graveyard sat just off the dirt-track road, with a tiny chapel standing in the middle of the many graves.

Nicolas steered the horse and buggy through the graveyard's narrow gates. Then he reined in the horse and the four of us climbed out.

Isobel hiked up the hem of her dress and took off across the graves, ignoring the narrow tracks that ran between them. Martin, Pepper and I followed. She came to a halt shortly afterwards at what was most certainly the newest grave.

'The stone was erected only last week,' said Isobel. 'I was here to support Vincenzio. He was completely and utterly devastated.'

Martin stared at the words carved into the stone.

BETHANY VIRGINIA CREWE PRECIO
1841–1866
Beloved Wife of Vincenzio

Isobel clung to Martin's arm as he studied the grave, his face blank. Then he gently shook her away and turned to walk back to the buggy.

I looked at the gravestone for a moment longer, then

both Pepper and I turned to follow Martin.

Isobel remained for a few more minutes. She said a prayer and crossed herself before returning to the buggy.

'Now I want to see the doctor,' said Martin.

'I've invited him to join us this evening for dinner,' said Isobel.

# 8

The doctor arrived promptly at six that evening, and he was ushered into the reception room by Nicolas.

I was waiting there with Pepper, Martin and Vincenzio.

'May I introduce Dr Edward Brewster,' Vincenzio said. He stood and shook the doctor's hand. And then Brewster hugged Vincenzio, which showed me that they were old friends.

'This is Mr and Mrs Pepper,' Isobel told Edward, 'and Beth's brother, Martin Crewe.'

'I'm pleased to meet you,' said Edward. 'And sorry for your loss. It was a shock to us all.'

'I must speak with you …' Martin said.

'Of course! Let's go into the sitting room and speak privately.'

Edward led Martin away, and Pepper and I remained with Isobel and Vincenzio in order to give him the privacy he needed.

'Madeira?' Isobel offered.

Nicolas had remained, and he now picked up the decanter and poured the wine into four goblets.

He served Isobel and me first, then Vincenzio and

Pepper. The doctor returned a few moments later.

'Where's Martin?' I asked.

'He needs a moment alone,' said Edward, and then he turned to Vincenzio. 'Why did you tell him Beth died of malaria?'

'Surely she did have malaria,' Isobel interjected.

'No,' said Edward. 'We found her dead one morning at the bottom of the dungeon steps.'

Isobel gasped in shock.

'It *was* malaria …' Vincenzio said.

Edward looked intently into his friend's face. Then Vincenzio Precio slumped.

'Vincenzio!' cried Isobel, running to help as Edward caught him.

'Let's get him to his room. He's not a well man.'

With the aid of Nicolas, Edward and Isobel helped Vincenzio from the room.

A few minutes later, Edward returned, accompanied by a subdued Martin. 'I was afraid of this,' the doctor said. 'Vincenzio is in denial. He found Beth's body. His mental health has been sorely tried ever since. I don't know why he made up that story about malaria. Perhaps it was easier for him to believe than what really happened.'

'What did happen?' asked Pepper. 'Did she fall down the dungeon steps?'

'No. There were no injuries. It was as though she had walked down there and simply dropped dead. I suspect it was some inherent heart condition.'

'Beth was always a very healthy child,' Martin said. 'I know of no illness she "inherited" that could explain her sudden death.'

Edward placed his hand on Martin's shoulder as he approached and then stopped by the fire. 'I'm sorry.

Sometimes we just can't explain these things. Modern science has an answer for many things, but not always why someone has died.'

Isobel returned. She looked pale and concerned.

'Vincenzio is sleeping,' she said. 'I don't understand what's happened here. He told me she had a sickness …'

'I believe it is easier for him to accept that than the truth,' said Edward. 'For now, anyway.'

Nicolas came back into the reception room. He looked surlier than usual. 'Dinner is served.'

'I don't feel very hungry right now,' Isobel said.

'We must all keep up our strength,' Pepper said. 'You'll be no use to your brother if you get sick too.'

'I suppose you're right. I'll do the best I can to eat,' Isobel said. 'You must eat too, Martin. For your own and your friends' sake.'

Then she took Martin's arm and led him away to the dining-room. Dr Brewster and Pepper followed. I remained in the reception room a moment longer.

Something was very wrong with the Precio household. I wasn't yet certain what it was, but I had a gut feeling that we would all soon be finding out.

'Kat?' called Pepper over his shoulder. 'Are you joining us?'

A piercing cry woke me, and I leapt once more from my bed to find Pepper already by the door. This was becoming a bit of a habit.

'What was that?' I wondered.

'A cry of utter torment,' said Pepper. 'But I believe we are being entertained again.'

'Entertained?'

'Yes. Some more dungeon fiction by our host,

perhaps?'

'Surely not! When the truth of Beth's death has just been revealed ...'

Pepper looked back at the door as another cry echoed through the air.

'We had better investigate,' I said. 'After all, that's what we do best.'

The cry came again just as we reached the iron gates under the staircase. Pepper tugged at the door, finding it locked this time.

'It just confirms this isn't a proper dungeon,' I commented. 'A real one would be sound-proofed so as not to disturb the castle's occupants.'

'This place has struck me as a folly from the beginning,' agreed Pepper. 'The castle exterior with high walls apparently designed not to keep something out, but to keep something in. The odd noises in the night. The unfriendly manservant. The perfect sister taking care of her obviously insane brother. And this dungeon under the stairs. It's all a little ...'

'Contrived? This whole place is like ... a stage, set for our amusement. I think that Martin even made that observation earlier.'

'Exactly.'

'What's going on?' asked Edward Brewster, now joining us at the door. The doctor had earlier accepted Isobel's invitation to spend the night at the castle.

Pepper did not reply, but opened his lock-picking kit and set to work with it. Within a few short seconds he had the door open.

Brewster, I noted, took Pepper's lock-picking abilities totally in his stride. It gave me the feeling that he had seen many extraordinary things in his life already. I was tempted to ask him, but resisted.

Through the gates, three torches lit the entranceway, and the light spilled down the stone steps. Without another word, the three of us hurried forward.

Halfway down, I brushed past a tapestry that I hadn't noticed the previous night because it had hung flush against the wall. This time, though, I could feel a breeze billowing around the tapestry, one corner of which appeared to be attached to the wall somehow. The light from above barely reached it, but I pulled the tapestry aside and discovered a hidden doorway in the brickwork behind it. The door had been wedged ajar with the tapestry corner.

Pepper and Brewster were a few steps ahead of me.

'Wait! Look at this,' I called.

They both stopped and came back up the steps to see what I had found. I used my sunpan to illuminate the scene. We could see the scarred stone where the edges of the hidden entrance met with the thick walls.

Pepper and Brewster wedged their fingers into the small gap and began to tug at the door. It opened.

A loud cry pierced the air, and it was obvious that it came from the space beyond the door. It paralysed Brewster for a moment, but made Pepper and me more determined to find out who had made it and where it came from.

It was pitch black beyond the door, the corridor torchlight not penetrating that far, so I aimed my sunpan bracelet into the gloom. Following my lead, Pepper held his pocket watch aloft, allowing the illuminated dial to shed some extra light.

'What is that?' Brewster asked, admiring my bracelet.

'A portable flameless torch,' I said.

There were five steps going down. I set off first, with Pepper and Brewster at my heels, and quickly came to a short corridor. The sunpan light filled the space, and we saw now a slightly open door ahead of us. A crack of light filtered though from beyond. I paused and glanced at Pepper, and we silently agreed that we would creep up on this new space, and hopefully find both the person who was in trouble and their tormentor. My hand went into the hidden pocket in my breeches and withdrew my small pistol, but I kept it down out of sight so that Brewster wouldn't be alarmed and shout out.

The door ahead opened wider, and I began to raise my hand. Then Vincenzio appeared on the threshold.

'What are you doing here?' he asked.

'We heard screaming. Coming from here,' Pepper said.

'What is going on here, Vincenzio?' asked Brewster.

'This is just the machine. My father's machine.'

'But we heard a scream,' I insisted. 'It sounded like a woman in pain.'

'I have to oil the mechanism, so that it doesn't seize up,' Vincenzio said, as though that explained everything.

'What mechanism?' I asked.

'The clock. It is the most accurate you'll ever find: a perfectly-made piece of machinery.'

'Clock?' said Brewster. 'What clock?'

'I'll show you ...'

We followed Vincenzio through the door, and found ourselves inside the base of a high tower that must have extended right up to the castle ramparts. A rickety wooden staircase zigzagged up the furthest wall to a narrow platform that afforded access to an intricate mechanism driving an immense clock.

The moment was surreal. I experienced a feeling of *déjà vu* as I recalled the dream I'd had on my first night in the castle. I turned in a circle while looking up. The clock-face was set into one side of the tower, while its workings stretched halfway across the space above.

'You can see this clock tower only if you approach the castle from the east,' Vincenzio explained.

'I suppose that is why I have never noticed it before,' said Brewster.

'And also why we didn't see it, as we travelled in from the west,' I said.

'My father made clocks for the joy of it,' Vincenzio continued, 'and this was his finest achievement. The mechanism needs to be regularly maintained, though, or it makes that awful sound that you mistook for screaming. It needs a lot of cleaning and oiling. And, because I suffer from insomnia, I find it soothing to work on it during the night.'

Vincenzio's face became animated as he talked about the clock, showing his true passion for this incredible piece of machinery.

'It's beautiful,' Pepper said. 'Martin would love to see this.'

'At least that explains the engine grease,' I said. 'On the hinges of the door above.'

'Yes I like to keep them well oiled,' Vincenzio said. 'This castle is full of strange noises at night. None of which are unexplainable. I tried to tell Beth this, but she …'

Vincenzio stopped speaking and his expression went blank. Then he rubbed his forehead and closed his eyes.

'I have a headache. You'll excuse me …'

'Perhaps I can give you something to help with that?' said Brewster.

We left the secret tower and returned to the reception hall of the castle. Brewster helped Vincenzio back to his room, and Pepper and I sat down together on the sofa by the dying embers of the fire while we waited for his return.

'What do you make of all this?' I asked Pepper.

'Vincenzio is very peculiar. Whenever he talks of Beth he … I'm not quite sure how to describe it, but he blanks out.'

'Yes,' I said. 'Then he has those moments of animation. The clock is obviously very important to him.'

'Mmmm. Perhaps it is the only thing that takes his mind from his wife's death.'

'Martin and Isobel haven't emerged from their rooms, despite the commotion,' I noted. 'Is it possible they didn't hear it?'

'I was wondering about that myself. I think we need to question Brewster on his relationship with Vincenzio. They were very friendly when the doctor arrived.'

As if he had been waiting for us to finish talking, Brewster then came back to the reception room.

'Vincenzio's sleeping now,' he said. 'I gave him a little laudanum. He's been through a lot these past months. I suppose we ought all to try to get some sleep now.'

'Soon,' I said. 'But first we'd like to ask you a few questions, doctor.'

'Very well. I will answer what I can.' Brewster sat down on the chair opposite us.

'How long have you known Vincenzio?'

Brewster frowned, then slow blinked. 'We have known each other for years. I forget how many. Socially at first. Vincenzio's father held many parties in this castle.'

'That's strange,' I said. 'Didn't Vincenzio live and study in England? I mean, why would he have been at those parties?'

Brewster slow blinked again.

'He always came back for holidays …'

'He and Isobel?' Pepper asked.

'Isobel?' said Brewster.

'Vincenzio's sister …' I said.

'Oh yes, of course. Yes *she* was always there too.'

We asked the doctor a few more questions but didn't learn much more, as he claimed client confidentiality. He then retired for the night.

'Penny for them …?' Pepper said after Brewster had left us.

'I was just thinking how hard it is for us two to turn off our natural suspicion of everyone and everything.'

'You think there is nothing odd going on here?'

'I think there is something odd going on everywhere. That's the point. Maybe this time there really is nothing more sinister than a grieving widower who has slightly lost his mind along with his wife.'

'Let's sleep on it, Kat,' said Pepper. 'It's been a long week and we may be forgiven for our suspicions, considering all that we know about this world.'

# 9

The next morning, before breakfast, feeling the need for exercise, I took a walk in the castle grounds. As I walked through the courtyard, past the stables, and carried on around to the back, I discovered that there was a huge garden and a maze. This was all within the castle walls.

I have confidence in my sense of direction, so I entered the maze without fear of becoming lost. I'd left Pepper back in our room, attending to his ablutions behind the screen, because I just needed some air.

The maze was beautifully designed, with ornate statues and healthy, well-watered, decorative plants as features in each of the dead ends. It took me around 15 minutes to get to the centre of the maze. There I found a magnificent stone sundial with a golden face. I went up to it and discovered it was almost seven o'clock. Then I heard a giggle that made me look around.

A small alcove of bushes was just off the centre, and there I found Martin and Isobel. Within the last few days they appeared to have grown very close. Martin was holding Isobel's hand and looking intently into her eyes. Why hadn't I spotted their interest in each other earlier?

I hurried away before they noticed they had been

observed, but I'll admit I did have a smile on my face. After the loss of his sister, and for all the hard work he did in the cause of demon-slaying, Martin deserved to find someone to make him happy. Didn't we all deserve more than this constant battle against evil that we had taken up?

I walked back to the castle, considering my relationship with Pepper and how it had almost become more than the strong friendship and trust we had previously shared.

I looked down at the ring on my hand – it was sitting too comfortably there – and thought again how odd it was that Pepper had just happened to have it on his person at the right moment. The thought gave me butterflies in my stomach: a sensation I'd had before when I was deeply infatuated with Pepper because of a vampire spell that made him irresistible to women: especially female vampires. I had tried not to look back on those days since the spell had been broken, or to recall the hurt expression in Pepper's eyes when I had given him back his ring.

I paused, looking up at the castle walls. From this angle I could see the clock tower attached to the east wing. Our room was on the other side, facing out over the front wall, or else I would have seen the maze and gardens sooner, from our window. I felt a compulsion to look carefully at the back windows, as if I suspected Pepper would be there looking out at me. He wasn't, of course, but as my gaze swept from one blank window to the next, I abruptly saw Vincenzio framed there, and the expression on his face seemed to be one of ugly rage.

I put my head down and hurried back toward the courtyard. What on earth had I done to upset Vincenzio so much? Perhaps he didn't like anyone going into his gardens without first asking. I realised that I owed the man a sincere apology.

'Miss. *Miss* …'

I turned to see who was calling me, and saw a gaunt, untidy man looking out at me from the stable.

'Yes?' I said.

'When are we *leaving*?'

I realised with some considerable shock that the man before me was our driver, Carlos. He appeared ragged, and so unkempt and thin that I hadn't recognised him.

'Carlos? What on earth …?'

'Miss, we need to get away, as soon as possible,' the man said.

I took a step back, because his eyes blazed with what could only be described as desperation or insanity.

'What has happened to you?' I said. 'Didn't the servants give you a bed? *Feed* you?'

'Yes miss, at first, but that was ten days ago. Evil lives here, Miss Lightfoot. And I think you know how to help. We have to escape. I tried … but I kept getting *confused*.'

'What do you mean *ten* days? This is only our third day here? Are you sick?' I said. 'Speak up, man.'

Carlos stepped back into the shadows of the stable.

'You don't know …' he said.

'Know what?'

'The *Xana*, Miss Lightfoot …'

'*Kat!*'

I turned to find Martin walking briskly toward the stable. I glanced back to Carlos but found that he had scurried away.

'I spotted you leaving the maze,' Martin said.

'Yes. It's a lovely garden and a beautiful maze.'

I was a little disconcerted by my exchange with Carlos, but something stopped me from telling Martin about it. For the first time ever, I felt as though I couldn't trust him.

I realised that my disconcerting encounter with Carlos, coupled with my sight of Vincenzio's angry expression, had kindled a sense of paranoia within me.

'I've fallen in love with Isobel,' he said. 'I feel like I've known her for longer than a few days.'

I was taken aback by Martin's direct words – they somehow fed my paranoia. I became suspicious and wondered if he had fallen victim to a spell. It was uncanny that just a few moments earlier I had been remembering the one put on Pepper and me.

'I'm … happy for you,' I said, opting for caution.

A prickle of anxiety worked its way along the back of my neck, and I fought the urge to look back up at the castle windows. I was certain that Vincenzio would be staring at us, and inexplicably believed that he already knew about Isobel and Martin and wasn't happy about it at all. Though why it should concern him, I didn't know.

'Walk back inside with me,' I suggested. 'Breakfast will be ready soon, and I'm sure Pepper would like to hear your news.'

I led Martin away from the stable, but glanced back to see Carlos peering out at us from inside. His eyes pleaded with me to rescue him. But I didn't understand what he needed saving from, even though my own suspicions had been heightened by his obvious terror and by the sudden change in Martin's behaviour.

We entered the castle through the courtyard door, and here is the thing – I realised at that moment that this appeared to be the only way in or out. I thought it odd that there were no rooms leading through patio doors directly onto the garden – at least, none that I had been in so far.

Martin walked directly through the reception room toward the dining-room, but I paused to look up at the impressive staircase, the large landing. I knew that there were two wings off the landing, which meant that the building sprawled far more extensively than I had so far explored.

Off the reception room was a small sitting room – that was where Martin had gone to have his private talk with Dr Brewster – but I hadn't been in there yet either. Beyond the dining-room I knew was the kitchen area, and servants' quarters too, but they surely couldn't account for the whole of the rest of the space on the castle's ground floor. And then something else occurred to me: Nicolas and one other man were the only servants I'd seen since my friends and I had arrived. Where were all the other staff an estate this size would need in order to run? Who watered the plants in the maze, and trimmed the bushes to keep them in their immaculate state? Who maintained the sprawling garden and lawns? Who made the delicious food we ate at every meal time?

'Kat?' called Martin from the door of the dining-room.

'Sorry … I was just wondering if anyone had called Pepper down for breakfast, or if I should …'

'Nicolas will fetch him,' said Isobel, appearing at Martin's shoulder. 'Good morning, Kat.'

Isobel looked beautiful, radiant even, in a red velvet dress that would be far too heavy for the heat outside, but was perfect for the cooler interior of the castle. Had she been wearing that dress in the maze? I couldn't remember.

'Martin?' she said, and he went to her, took her hand and kissed it. Then they walked into the dining-room together.

I followed them, and sat down opposite them at the table in my usual place. Vincenzio hadn't joined us, and neither had the doctor. I supposed that our late-night excursions had left them both tired. Pepper, Martin and I were all accustomed to having little sleep, and so didn't need much of it to feel refreshed.

Pepper came in, followed by Nicolas, who then went off to the kitchens through the door at the far end of the room.

Pepper sat next to me and looked at Martin, frowning.

Martin was gazing into Isobel's eyes.

The couple broke from their reverie only when Nicolas came in carrying a tray of food. Fresh-cooked eggs, still-warm bread and sizzling bacon were laid before us. I realised I was famished, and eagerly helped myself to the food on the tray. Then I remembered the ravaged state of our coachman, Carlos.

'Nicolas,' I said. 'How is Carlos faring?'

'Carlos?' he replied, and then he looked at Isobel. An odd expression crossed his face, and then he smiled slightly. 'Your coachman? Ah, he is sick. I asked Dr Brewster to go and see him this morning.'

'What's wrong with him?' I said.

'Some kind of fever. I'm sure he will be well soon.'

'Good, because we will have to leave very soon,' said Pepper. 'Won't we, Martin?'

'*Leave?*' said Martin, and he turned to look at Pepper. 'I'm not ready to leave.'

Pepper and I exchanged a glance. I could see Pepper was as baffled as I was by Martin's odd behaviour.

'I'll explain later ...' I mouthed to him, when Martin and Isobel began to gaze into each other's eyes again.

'How is your brother this morning?' Pepper asked Isobel.

'My brother?' she replied vaguely, as though she couldn't remember who Vincenzio was. Then she turned her pure bright blue eyes toward us. 'Dr Brewster has taken him away from the castle for a few days,' she said. 'A change of scenery is just what he needs to make him … feel better.'

'When did they leave?' I asked. 'Only, I thought I saw him earlier.'

'They went around 6.00 am, so I doubt you would have seen him.'

'I see. I must have been mistaken,' I said. 'Do you mind if I show Pepper the garden after breakfast?'

'Not at all,' said Isobel. Then she returned her gaze to Martin.


'This is lovely,' Pepper said when we reached the maze.

This far from the castle, I was certain that we wouldn't be overheard. I linked Pepper's arm, mimicking the newlywed behaviour that I thought our hostess or Nicholas would expect if they were watching us, but it also helped me to draw Pepper closer, so that I could speak to him in low tones.

I told him about my encounter with Carlos, and about noticing Vincenzio at the window before that. It was unlikely that Vincenzio and Dr Brewster could have left the castle since then without us seeing them.

'I feel like I'm watching a play and the plot keeps changing,' I said. 'I mean, you heard Nicolas say that Brewster had gone to check on Carlos, didn't you?'

'Yes,' Pepper said. 'And this sudden infatuation between Martin and Isobel … It's out of character for Martin. I suspect for both of them.'

'Mmmm. I agree.'

'Why don't we walk around the maze a little, do the show of being in love, and then try exploring the rest of the grounds?' Pepper suggested.

Pepper stopped me just at the opening of the maze and, turning me to face him, kissed my hand. I glanced back at the castle as he did this, feeling certain that eyes were on us. But my fleeting look was insufficient to confirm if anyone lurked at the windows. When I looked back at Pepper, I saw a brief expression pass across his face, and then he smiled at me like a doting husband. I smiled back, then on impulse placed a kiss on his cheek.

A tiny flush coloured his cheeks, and I realised that perhaps I had overdone the loving wife act a little.

Taking his arm once more, I led him into the maze.

# 10

I left Pepper at the sundial and went to explore the small alcove where Martin and Isobel had been earlier. There was a low stone bench there and an array of vibrant plant-life that made it a perfect setting for a romantic encounter. Too perfect, almost. I shrugged, then turned to leave. That was when I noticed a peculiarity. Part of the maze wall appeared to be made up not of shrubbery but of rock.

'Pepper?'

Pepper came over and took a look. 'It's a boulder of some kind,' he said. 'Odd place to put it.'

'Yes. It is. Let's check out the other alcoves …'

We made our way back through the maze, going into the dead ends deliberately this time, and at each point we found one of these weird boulders.

'I wish I could see this maze from above,' Pepper said. 'I wonder what arrangement these stones are placed in, and if it has any particular significance?'

'It is odd to have them here like this,' I said. 'Perhaps we need to reconsider our priority in this exploration?'

'We do,' Pepper agreed.

Instead of searching around the grounds and exterior as we had originally planned, we returned to the castle and climbed the stairs.

'I believe that Vincencio's rooms are this way,' Pepper said. 'Let's see if Isobel was telling the truth about his absence.'

'Yes,' I agreed, 'her sudden announcement of his departure seemed very contrived – especially as I had seen him only minutes before …'

I didn't ask how Pepper knew where Vincenzio's room was, but trusted that he had found out for some reason.

We passed our own room and came to a door on the right.

'This makes sense,' I said. 'His window would be overlooking the garden and maze.'

Pepper knocked on the door. '*Don* Vincenzio?' he called.

There was no answer, and after we had waited a respectable time, Pepper retrieved his lock-picking kit from his pocket and set to work that morning. I meanwhile kept a lookout; but the castle was unusually quiet. I suspected Martin was occupied somewhere with Isobel, and I hadn't seen Nicolas or the other manservant since breakfast.

The lock clicked as it turned, and Pepper quickly opened the door. I looked inside, to see to my surprise that the room was devoid of furnishings.

'This can't be Vincenzio's room,' I said. 'We've made a mistake somehow.'

Pepper shook his head. 'I saw him enter on our first night here. While you were preparing for bed, I went out into the corridor. He even wished me goodnight.'

I entered the room and approached the window. My boots clacked on the wooden floor, the sound echoing in the empty room.

'We can see the garden from here,' I said, pleased that I had been right about that. 'It's possible that this was his wife's room. He may have rid himself of Beth's possessions after she died …'

'I suppose,' said Pepper, following me to the window.

I looked down over the maze and garden.

'There,' said Pepper. 'Look …'

He pointed out the stones to me. From within the twists and turns of the maze their positioning had seemed random, but from here, with the benefit of an aerial view, the pattern was unmistakable.

'It's as I thought,' said Pepper. 'The stones are in a circle. Probably an ancient place of worship. Vincenzio must have had the maze built around it.'

'Fascinating,' I said. 'But why not remove the stones?'

'Superstition, perhaps?'

'What now?'

'We go and search the castle as planned. This time from the inside. Then maybe we will explore the perimeter this afternoon.'


The downstairs was pretty much as I had expected it to be. Because we hadn't been in there so far, we headed first to the drawing room. It was a small but comfortable room with a harpsichord in one corner, a card table, and plush chairs around the hearth. On the walls were hung several painted portraits. One I recognised as Vincenzio and the other I realised was Bethany Precio. She did bear a vague resemblance to me, in as much as we had the same colouring and build. But Beth's eyes were very like Martin's, and the resemblance was impossible to miss.

After looking in this room, we explored the large

reception area. There appeared to be no rooms other than those we had already been into. Everywhere else was bricked up. Pepper even looked behind the huge wall tapestries, but there were no other doorways, hidden or otherwise.

'It doesn't make any sense,' Pepper said.

'Let's check out the kitchen. Maybe there are lots of other rooms beyond it.'

I entered the dining-room, half expecting to find Martin and Isobel still sitting at the table where we had left them. But there was no sign of them at all. They hadn't been in any of the other rooms downstairs, and I had no idea where they were now.

'Perhaps he's resting in his room?' I said.

'Or maybe they went to the graveyard again …'

'It's possible.'

I reached the kitchen door before Pepper did, and as I opened it, Nicolas appeared in front of me.

'Can I help you?' he asked.

'We wanted to see the kitchen,' I said, 'and to congratulate your cook on the very nice food we've been served.'

'I'll pass on your thanks,' said Nicolas.

He stayed in the doorway, barring our entrance.

'Can't we tell her ourselves?' Pepper said.

'This area is not open to guests,' Nicolas said, in his usual surly manner. 'You may ask *Doña* Isobel if you can go inside, but until she says so, there is no entry for you.'

'What if we ask *Don* Vincenzio?' I said. 'Surely he wouldn't mind.'

Nicolas blinked slowly, and I was immediately reminded of Edward Brewster's same slow blink the night before, as though he had had to give himself time to work out his response to our questions.

'As *Doña* Isobel told you, *Don* Vincenzio is not here right now. He left with the doctor,' said Nicolas.

'And what of Carlos? Did the doctor see him before he left?'

Nicolas smiled very slowly. 'Oh yes. Your coachman was much better: he took the doctor and *Don* Vincenzio on their trip.'

Pepper asked Nicolas where they had gone, but the servant refused to answer and turned back into the kitchen. As the door closed behind him, I managed to glance over his shoulder, and saw a long corridor that led off somewhere, but nothing more.

Then I heard a bolt slide into place, and knew that this time Pepper's lock-picking skills would be of no use.

A little while later, *sans* bulky skirt, I walked with Pepper back toward the garden. We stopped by the stable to check on the status of Carlos and our carriage, and sure enough both of them were gone.

'There's not even a stable hand here,' I commented. 'How is this place even functioning with so little visible staff?'

I had observed that every day when we returned to our room the bed was made and the fire lit. The room was always dust-free and clean, too. But never did we see the servants who took care of this for us.

I looked around the interior of the stable. There were the usual things that one might expect to find, including a smelting fire, a saddle hung over the central wall between two horse stalls, which also had clean hay on the floors, and a filled water trough. A set of horse grooming brushes were laid out on a tidy work surface: they looked new.

I was struck again by how the stable, like the castle rooms, appeared ever-ready on the surface but showed little sign of actually being used. What was going on here? Was this turning into a mystery that even we wouldn't be able to solve?

There was no sign of the open buggy that had taken us to the graveyard, or of the horse that had pulled it, though everything in the stable implied that they were kept there, at least sometimes. And what of Carlos? Hadn't he used the stalls to feed and rest his horses at least? If he had, then why was there no evidence of it?

I met Pepper outside, where he had been walking the stable's perimeter while I explored inside.

'Come and see this,' he said.

I followed him around the back of the stable, where he pointed out to me that it had a solid stone wall that curved around and adjoined the side of the castle. Evidently the stable was not an outbuilding made of wood, as it had appeared to be from the front, but was in fact a part of the castle structure. An extension to it, one might say.

At the back of the castle, we were greeted by the sight of a sheer wall. No windows or doors opening into the kitchens we knew lay beyond, and no windows for any of the rooms that had to be on the upper floors.

Then we came to the tower exterior, and the clock-face above testified to its positioning in the structure.

'It doesn't make sense,' said Pepper. 'The exterior doesn't match the interior.' And then he voiced all of my own concerns about the castle layout and what really lay behind this sheer wall.

'Maybe this is actually the exterior wall that we thought circled the estate,' I suggested. 'And the castle, with kitchen and bedroom windows, is behind it.'

'If so, then it's very bizarre architecture,' Pepper said. 'I mean, there really appears to be only one way in and one way out.'

'That thought struck me this morning.'

'No designer would ever do that,' Pepper said. 'There always have to be other exits, in case of a fire or something.'

I didn't know what to make of it at all. There wasn't any apparent crime being committed, nor anything we could attribute to demonic activity. Nor did Bethany Precio's death appear suspicious. That was, if Edward Brewster's recounting of events was to be believed; and I had no reason to be suspicious of him at all.

However, the doctor's sudden disappearance with Vincenzio was concerning, as was their procurement of Carlos and his coach. For it meant we three were certainly stuck here until they returned: a convenient situation for Martin, at least, in his blossoming romance with Isobel.

We walked back to the castle entrance and went inside in silence.

A tray of appetising sandwiches and cakes, with a decanter of Madeira, was waiting for us on a table that had been placed between two comfortable chairs by the fire.

'I can't believe the morning has flown by so quickly,' Pepper said. 'I'll go to Martin's room and see if he's there.'

'Don't you think I should come with you?' I asked.

'No, that's okay. I won't be long. I'll bring him down and we'll talk our findings through with him.'

I felt a prickle of anxiety at the thought of revealing what little we knew to Martin, but squashed the suspicion as soon as it came into my mind. Martin had always been trustworthy. How many times had he or his inventions been responsible for saving our lives at the eleventh hour?

Why did I suddenly mistrust him? It just didn't make sense.

Pepper took the stairs two at a time, and I sat down in one of the chairs by the fire. I regarded the wine, considering whether or not I wanted some. I would have preferred tea. I was considering pulling the call bell by the fire when Martin came in from the dining-room.

'Ah, Martin, Pepper has just gone to look for you.'

'Really? I thought you two were having a jolly time exploring without me,' he said.

'What do you mean? We went for a walk …'

'Kat, it's me you're talking to. I know what you two were doing. But what I don't understand is why?'

'I'm not sure …'

'What's with you two? You haven't relaxed since we arrived here. Then you're sneaking around in men's clothing looking for an adventure.'

'Martin, I'm sorry. But things just don't add up here,' I said. 'You must see that? Even through a love-tinted monocle?'

I looked up and saw Pepper coming downstairs with Isobel.

'So, how long will they be gone?' he said.

'A few days at the most,' Isobel replied. 'Dr Brewster believed that the arrival of Bethany's brother had triggered a breakdown in my brother. He's taken him away to give him a little respite and medication to try to calm his nerves.'

'It sounds very serious,' Pepper said. 'Very difficult for you also.'

'I'd *rather* Vincenzio was away right now. He wasn't coping well. And I fear for his long-term health.'

Martin pulled up two more chairs around the table by the fire, and he poured us all a glass of Madeira. He held one of the glasses out to me – and I took it, but didn't drink from it – and then one to Isobel.

The atmosphere had suddenly changed with the return of Isobel and Pepper. I was feeling a great deal of sympathy and compassion for Isobel and Vincenzio, and a considerable amount of guilt over my suspicion of her.

Even so, my logical mind caused me to question my rather sudden change of heart, when just minutes before I had desperately wanted to find Martin and leave. Now we were all having a rather civilised lunch.

I reached for a small tea plate and placed a few of the sandwiches on it. I was hungry, and that surprised me in view of the large breakfast we'd had that morning. I nibbled one of the sandwiches. It contained shredded duck, beautifully seasoned, and the bread was freshly-baked, light and delicious.

'This was Beth's favourite,' Martin said.

'I know,' said Isobel. 'I thought you might enjoy it also.'

Martin smiled at Isobel, and Pepper caught my eye while they were both distracted by each other. Pepper was smiling at me too, and there was definitely something in the air, because I found myself returning his smile.

# 11

I had almost forgotten everything that had happened that morning: the disturbing encounter with Carlos in the stable; the searching of the castle; the discovery of Vincenzio's empty room; Nicolas's refusal to let us pass into the kitchens; and the peculiar design of the building. We spent a beautiful afternoon in the gardens. Martin and Isobel walked hand in hand, and their romance rubbed off on Pepper and me.

At first I thought my companion was merely playing his role to perfection, but then I felt that familiar flip flop in the pit of my stomach and realised that I was enjoying his attention and the scenario we found ourselves in.

It was nice to relax for a while. The realisation that we were stuck at the castle for a few days more no longer dismayed me. I should have been worrying about it. I wanted us to return home and resume our lives, and yet another part of me didn't. The castle was a haven from the rest of the world. It was safe. I was here with my friends, and other than the rather surly Nicolas, nothing could mar this visit. Or could it?

After dinner, Pepper and I returned to our room holding hands. It didn't feel uncomfortable or awkward, it seemed perfectly natural, and I had begun to believe that we were the newlyweds we were pretending to be.

We entered our room, and I went immediately to the screen to change out of the blue velvet dress I was wearing. Pepper sat on the edge of the bed, waiting for me. When I came back around, now in my nightwear, it struck me that this was a very different night from all the others when we had innocently shared a room. I wanted Pepper to kiss me. And why wouldn't he? We were married now, and so …

My mind halted. Married? No … We weren't. Why had I thought that?

Pepper stood and approached me. His hands rested on my shoulders, and he looked down into my eyes, letting the true depth of feeling he had for me come forward. I knew the truth then. For him, this was a dream come true. Here, sheltered in the castle, we could be anything we wanted to be. We could live life without fear. We could forget about the evil that threatened to take over the world outside.

My heart skipped a beat as he bent to kiss me. Then, when his lips touched mine, I knew something else. This was what I wanted too.

I stepped back and away from him. Pepper's arms fell to his side. His face showed grief at my rejection, and my heart shattered. The pain was real. My heart's desire was before me. Why couldn't I let this go where it needed to go?

We'd been through so much together.

'Think about it,' I murmured.

Pepper frowned. He was confused by my words.

'All that we've seen. All that we've shared. All that we know.'

His frown deepened, and then his brow smoothed out.

I knew he was indeed recalling all that had happened since we had met just a few years ago.

'I love you,' he said. 'But something definitely isn't right here.'

His words brought that fearful pain and genuine excitement. For a moment I concentrated on his declaration of love and nothing else. I was slipping again, and I moved back into his arms.

He embraced me, but made no more attempt to kiss me.

'You were right. Think, Kat. Think about our lives, our home.'

My mind fell back into the past, and I clung to the essence of myself. Clung to the strong, demon-slaying woman I was, while part of my inner self embraced the truth of my feelings for Pepper.

*This* emotion wasn't fake, but our surroundings were.

'Time to find out the truth,' Pepper said.

I sighed. I didn't want to let him go. Part of me thought this might be the only real chance for happiness we would ever have. If I spurned it, if we went back to our reality, would I ever know this moment again?

Ever gentle, Pepper pushed me away. It was my turn to look hurt. My heart hurt so much that it was as though it were being pulled from my chest.

'Fight it,' said Pepper. 'Yes, it hurts, but I promise you this is not the end for us.'

I sighed again, taking in a cool breath, forcing my anxiety down.

'What has happened to us?' I choked.

'A spell.'

'I feel this. I really do,' I said, admitting the truth to him for the first time.

'I know. We both do. This thing has just brought it out

in us. Made it impossible to hide anymore.'

Shivering despite the warmth of the room, I returned to the screen and got back into my breeches and the loose-fitting shirt, although my heart wasn't in it.

'So, we get to the bottom of this? Once and for all?' Pepper said.

I walked back around the screen. He was waiting by the door. He looked awkward. I suspected that he too was fighting against a temptation to drop back into that illusory moment.

'How?' I asked.

'You know how. Something in this castle is affecting us, and Isobel and Martin too.'

'*Don* Vincenzio is some kind of demon?' I suggested. 'He's not left at all. Maybe he's hiding in his dungeon.'

'Possible. I just don't know. But we gather everyone together and tell them what we know. Maybe the true demon will reveal itself to us.'

'Maybe we should check out the dungeon first? If we unmask Vincenzio, it will make the explanation even easier.'

Pepper thought about this for a moment and then agreed.

I strapped on my weapons belt, and placed a silver dagger encrusted with diamond shards into the holster in my boot. Martin had made the dagger when we had discovered that some demons were allergic to silver and some to diamonds. I also had a new laser gun, which I took from my weapons carpetbag. The sunpan bracelet was on my wrist, and fully charged after our afternoon outside in the garden. Pepper had his semi-automatic pistol that fired both bullets and diamond shards, depending on the cartridge he loaded, and he filled his pockets with ammunition and spare armaments.

'Let's get to the bottom of this. Once and for all,' I said, echoing Pepper's earlier words.

Then Pepper opened the bedroom door and stepped out into the corridor. I followed.

But I was no longer in the east wing. I was in pitch darkness, and Pepper was nowhere to be seen.

# 12

I reached for my sunpan bracelet and twisted it on. The space lit up, and I discovered I was in a wide tunnel cut into pure rock. Pepper was gone.

Anxiety returned, along with adrenaline, and I stood up straight and tried to gather my thoughts.

Somehow I had moved from the castle to this cave and in the blink of an eye been separated from Pepper. I turned back to where our room should have been, wondering if we had passed through a hidden door: it wouldn't be the first time I had found secret passages in a large house, and a castle would be more likely to have them than most. However, there was no sign of anything other than rock walls to either side of me.

I decided I had to move on, try to find my way back and out of this place. I opted to go forward for now. One direction, especially when you didn't know where you were, was as good as another.

The tunnel widened briefly and then narrowed again. I continued on, even when the height reduced until I had to bend to pass through. The space became claustrophobic. I imagined that the walls were closing in on me, that any moment I would be crushed. Then the narrowing tunnel opened up before me.

I entered an impossible cavern. A deep and clear pool of what looked like water lay in the centre and was surrounded by vegetation that couldn't possibly have survived or grown underground. A breeze wafted from somewhere, and I looked up to see an opening in the roof and the stars glinting in the night sky above. The moon shone down into the cave, lighting the pool, which glinted as a gentle current moved the water.

There was the sound of tinkling bells on the wind, and then I began to wonder: had I crossed over once more into the fae realm? I had thought that the light and dark fae had finished with me[2], but maybe this was all some trickery wrought by their magic? What other explanation could there be? The fae could change a doorway, twisting the very aspect of dimensional space. I had seen it happen before.

I passed by the pool and glanced down to see a shoal of silver fish swimming just beneath the surface. The chirrup of crickets came from somewhere outside the cave. I looked around to see if I could find any way of climbing upwards and out through the wide opening above. Even if I had indeed stumbled out of my own world and into another, I knew there would be some way back. If only I could get out.

The cave expanded before me. A throne made of soft moss over stone was surrounded by a canopy of blossoming vines. Behind the throne, the canopy was draped over a large crag that glittered in the moonlight. It was purple crystal – amethyst, I think. Very beautiful, and hypnotic. The whole place had a magical gloss shining over it. Dazzling and spellbinding. I gazed at it for some

---

[2] See *Kat of Green Tentacles*

time, watching the twinkling of the moonlight that bounced off the pool and illuminated the crystal.

This *had* to be a fae domain. It was too perfect.

I carried on toward the throne, and my booted feet crushed a carpet of flowers. Then I heard a song. It was beautiful. Pure, high, ethereal notes floated around the cave. And then a waterfall started behind the throne, and it parted for me like a curtain being pulled back.

I was compelled to follow the song, and passed through the waterfall, which fell closed once more. I glanced back. The cavern behind me had changed. I was certain that it would no longer lead back to where I had come from, if I tried to turn back. But I didn't. I wanted to go forward. I took one step, then another, and I realised that my feet were now bare, and that a long, wide, flowing gown brushed my legs.

It was inconvenient, because now I would have to lift the hem to avoid stepping on it, instead of walking easily, unhampered in my britches.

When I did lift the hem, I saw that my legs were bare also. There were no undergarments, and the dress flowed around my legs as though I were some sea nymph risen from the waves.

Maybe I was imagining it, maybe not. The fae had all sorts of tricks up their sleeves, and held magic that our human minds would never fully comprehend. Even so, on the whole, they weren't evil, and so I rationalised that I had nothing to fear.

Besides: I had my weapons. My hand fell to my belt, but it too had disappeared along with my own clothing. Damn.

The cave darkened as I moved deeper inwards, and I realised that my sunpan bracelet was no longer on my wrist. I whistled, and the echoes came back to me, outlining a full-length mirror just ahead of me.

I walked toward the mirror, and the light brightened once more. I saw myself dressed in a flowing gown in rich purple. Without stockings or boots, the outfit felt decadent. And there were no underskirts to lift the hem and stop the fabric clinging to my thighs. It was a somewhat freeing sensation. The dress felt good as it flowed around my legs.

The song became more intense, and drew me away from the mirror.

Where was I headed?

I stopped moving, but the music grew louder and pulled my unwilling legs forward. I was unable to resist, and didn't know why.

Lights twinkled ahead of me. Filling the sky. But no, this was no sky, it was the ceiling of the cave.

And then I left the cavern and came into a ballroom.

The music was louder here, and the room was filled with people. Over in one corner was a group of musicians wearing carnival masks. A couple danced past me: a handsome man and a striking woman, both young and smiling with joy as though the night fulfilled all of their dreams for the future.

More beautiful couples passed, all wearing similarly happy expressions. I thought to stop one of them to ask where I was, but they spun by me so quickly. It was like watching a carousel at a travelling circus. Only these were not horses emulating galloping but people dancing.

Shocked, I saw Vincenzio, dancing with a stunning woman. The woman had the laughing eyes of Martin Crewe, and I recognised Beth from her portrait.

'She's not dead!' laughed Vincenzio as they twirled by. 'Haha! She's been here all this time!'

I saw Dr Brewster in the middle of the party too, his

arms around another beautiful woman. He was happy, and looked younger than he had appeared when I had last seen him. What was happening? Had I fallen and hit my head? Was I dreaming this insane scenario?

And our coach driver, Carlos, was there too, with a sprig of a girl who danced with the vitality of the very young.

This was bizarre. It had to be a dream. No way would any of these people be behaving so strangely in real life.

'This is where you are …' I said. 'Having fun while we all worried about you. Now that would be a nice story to be able to tell back home. But of course you are all completely in my imagination, aren't you?'

Saying this out loud did not make the truth present itself. No, the assembled people danced on.

*I'll pass through this area and wake up in my room, with Pepper sleeping soundly by my side*, I told myself.

I began to weave through the dancers. It was difficult, because they moved so fast. Had the Pied Piper taken hold of them through the music? Or were they all wearing magical shoes?

Vincenzio passed me again, and Beth looked so happy to be with him.

There was a buffet of food in the centre of the room, and the dancers moved around it.

'Why not stop a while?' I called to Vincenzio. 'Eat something? Then talk to me.'

But they danced on.

'Don't eat!' whispered one of the dancers as they twirled behind me.

'Don't drink!' said another.

I looked at the food. It was drawing me in, more interesting than the music, for certain.

'Dance with me, Kat,' said another voice behind me.

I turned and saw Pepper moving through the throng, dancing continually but without a partner.

'Eat. And then dance with me forever,' he said.

There was something about his movements and the forced smile on his lips that made me realise how very wrong this whole situation actually was.

Pepper was urging me to eat, even as the passing dancers begged me not to.

A goblet of wine appeared by my side as I stood at the table, and then it was in my hand. At that moment, Vincenzio and Beth swirled past me again, and the goblet was knocked from my hand.

'You can't escape,' said Beth, her smile now a grimace as she tried to fight whatever magic was holding her.

'Drink and join me,' said Pepper.

I felt that surge of emotion for him again. Pepper was here, trapped as the others were. How could I help them?

'Be with me,' Pepper said again, but even as his lips moved and his hand held out to me, I saw the pain and frustration in his eyes. He fought with himself until his movements slowed. He forced the smile from his lips and then spoke again.

'Drink … Don't … Kat … Don't … trust … anyone … even me.'

The music screeched and Pepper danced away. I followed him, and saw his hand waving to the back of the room and a row of mirrors.

'Run …' Pepper said. 'Through …'

I was now in a quandary. Pepper had said I was to trust no-one, not even him. Could this be another trap, or did he have enough control to show me the way out of this labyrinth of caves and fake ballrooms?

I walked toward the mirrors. The music screeched and wailed now. It had lost its ability to compel me: somehow

I had defeated its influence. Maybe with the assistance of some of those already caught in it.

'Kat, what are you doing there?' said Martin.

He was looking at me, wide-eyed, from the other side of one of the mirrors.

'Pepper told me to run through. Are you in the house?'

Martin looked around him. The room was dark behind and I couldn't make out his location.

'I don't know where I am,' he said. 'I'm lost.'

'Wait there. Don't move,' I said.

I moved on to the second mirror. This time I saw the castle garden. It was night and the stone circle was visible. The maze was no longer weaved in and around it.

I went back to Martin's mirror. 'What does a stone circle mean?'

'A stone circle?' He thought for a moment. 'There are many ancient circles around the world. They represent an old religion, paganism, but some also call them fairy rings, and they are thought to be the source of power for the fae.'

'If one of the stones was toppled,' I said, 'would that disperse the power?'

'I don't know. Perhaps.'

'Worth a try then,' I said. 'Don't worry. If my theory is right, everyone here will be freed shortly. Including you.'

I moved back to the second mirror and reached out to the glass with my fingers. It moved and rippled at my touch, as though it were nothing more than another waterfall that I could safely run through.

I stepped back and then, before my nerve gave, ran forward and leapt into the second mirror. As I came into contact with the liquid glass, I heard Pepper's cry behind me: 'Not that one, Kat!'

But it was too late.

As I had hoped, the glass didn't shatter. It became warm and fluid around me, and I fell through, tumbling down from a low height onto the lawn.

I rolled with the fall and came to a natural halt without really hurting myself.

I sat up, looking back to where the mirror doorway had been, but could see nothing. I was back in the castle grounds, but now they were much changed. The neatly-trimmed grass of the morning was massively overgrown, almost waist high: impossible for just one day of growth.

I stood up and looked around. As I had seen through the mirror, the stone circle was now visible, because the maze was gone. I walked toward it, ever wary of the fact that Pepper had called out a final warning as I had gone through the mirror. Maybe this wasn't really the castle garden at all, but something that resembled it in this mad and warped reality I had stumbled into. That at least would explain the disappearance of the maze and the suddenly long grass.

I reached the perimeter of the stone circle and then walked inside it, half expecting a barrage of fae magic to strike me to the ground.

'So, you're a fairy circle,' I said to the stones. 'Possibly the source of power that has taken control of my friends. What am I going to do with you?'

I leaned against one of the stones, pushing it to see if I could get it to move and possibly topple. But it was stuck fast. Nothing was going to move it; or, I discovered, any of the others. They appeared to be almost rooted in the ground.

I walked the interior of the circle, frequently tripping over the purple gown, until frustrated I ripped away the front hem, freeing the lower part of my legs. Then I used my feline agility to leap onto the top of one of the stones.

Crouched there, I looked down over the circle. I could see a flow of energy that passed from one stone to another. It reinforced it. The grass inside was short, unlike that surrounding, which almost clawed its way up the sides of the stones.

Martin had been right: the magic was here. But who was using it and why?

I looked back over the tall grass, in the direction of the castle, and noticed that the building was not there. Instead there was a large bulk of rock, roughly matching the height and shape of the castle. However, the clock tower remained. It was the only 'built' part of the rock, and it towered up, the clock-face illuminated by the moon.

I leapt down from the stone to the exterior of the circle and, lifting up the remnants of my skirt, ran toward the rock and the tower.

As before, there was no entrance from this side. I could see now that it was sheer rock face right up to the brick wall of the tower. A line of energy rolled around the clock-face, coming from the circle. It floated like mist from the stones.

I walked back toward the former courtyard. The stable shape was still there, only there was no stable, merely an empty cavern that protruded outwards where it had been.

Fae magic was strong, but I had not known that it could change the structure and shape of solid rock.

I glanced inside the structure and saw it was empty and abandoned, unlike earlier when it had been set for use. And of course this all made sense to me now. Pepper and I had been right: the castle was a stage, set for a performance. But I still did not know who was responsible, or why.

# 13

I gazed up at the rock, wondering how I could get back inside without the aid of magic. I wanted to get into the clock tower again and take a proper look at that mechanism. And then I remembered: there was a way inside – the entrance was through the courtyard.

I hurried away from the former stable and rounded the side of the rock. There was no courtyard as such now, merely a space of overgrown land. Moss grew on the rock-face, and the dried-out grass was tall brush, which I pushed my way through until I reached the entrance.

What had once appeared to be a doorway was now an arched, hooded bulge of rock with a gaping hole that led into the caves.

I glanced down at my arm, mourning the loss of my sunpan light bracelet; but that wouldn't stop me from seeing inside anyway. I still had my special talents, and I doubted the magic of my mystery opponent could take those away from me.

I entered the cave, giving a low whistle. The space was narrow, resembling the small foyer that led into the large reception room. It opened out into a high cave. Through my echo-location, I could see the shape of the stairs leading upwards, possibly carved by some ancient hand centuries ago, and underneath them a lip of rock: the open entrance that led toward the dungeon and the clock tower entrance.

I paused at the arch. There were no ornate iron gates now, just an unwelcoming hollow. Would this really lead me to the clock tower? And if it did, what would I find there?

'Kat, why don't you join us for supper?'

I turned around to see the reception room once more restored. Martin and Isobel sat by the fire, and the table with snacks and drinks lay before them.

'You look upset,' said Isobel. 'What is wrong?'

I glanced back toward the stairs. The castle structure was all there again. And the iron gates were closed and barred.

'This is lovely wine,' Martin said.

'Don't!' I warned, as he went to drink.

'What's gotten into you?' he asked.

'Don't drink or eat anything,' I said. 'It's not real. None of this is real.'

'What are you talking about?' Isobel said. 'This is my childhood home. You're safe here. Nothing can harm you. You haven't been listening to the servants' chatter about ghosts, have you? They love to tell those stories.'

'What servants? I only ever see Nicolas and one other – whose name escapes me, because he so rarely appears.'

'Matthias, you mean? My dear, you must have seen the gardeners and the stable hands, and the cook. Why, last night she came up because you insisted on seeing her,' Isobel said. 'Isn't that right Martin?'

Martin nodded. 'Yes. I was there. What's gotten into you, Kat?'

I began to doubt myself. The thought that my mind was inventing all that I had seen, and that I might be losing my sanity, was not an attractive one.

'Why, here is the cook again now,' said Isobel.

A portly woman came into the room with a tray of cakes. She wore a black dress with a pure white apron over it. There was a slight dusting of flour on the front of her hair.

'I thought you might like these,' she said.

She looked exactly as I would have imagined a Spanish cook to look just after baking a tray of cakes.

'You're not real,' I said. 'You're here for my sake, but I know you're not real.'

Martin frowned and reached for his goblet. I ran forward, knocking it from his hand. It fell to the floor, spilling a greenish-looking ichor all over the stone and shattering to pieces.

'Why did you do that?' asked Martin.

Then, as we looked on, the goblet repaired itself, the green slime was sucked back off the floor and Martin bent to pick it up. He did not place it to his lips, but put it down onto the table.

'There's something in the food, and in … whatever that stuff is, that is confusing you, Martin. It's making you susceptible to whatever is suggested. Neither you nor Isobel should partake of it.'

'You think we've been poisoned!' squealed Isobel. Her hands flew to her mouth.

The old cook had vanished now. Maybe she had merely left the room, returning to her kitchen, or maybe the magic that had created her had waned when the goblet fell.

'Look,' I said. 'Come with me to the clock tower. I have something to show you.'

Martin stood up immediately, but Isobel caught his arm.

'I'm scared,' she said. 'I have all of these memories of growing up here, but they feel like a dream ...'

I went to Isobel and touched her arm. She was solid enough, real. And I was sure Vincenzio had been too, and Beth when they had been dancing together. I knew Carlos was a real person, because he had driven us here all the way from Madrid.

'What do you remember before you arrived here?' I asked Isobel.

'I remember ... the letter. From Vincenzio. Telling me of Beth's death. Naturally I came.'

'New York,' said Martin. 'I received the letter about Beth. Then we got on a ship and made our way here.'

'Yes. That's right. Everything was normal. Until we arrived here, and then nothing seemed to add up,' I said. 'Right. I'm not letting anyone out of my sight. Come with me. We're going to the clock tower.'

'Why?' asked Martin.

'Because I think the answer to this mystery lies there.'

Martin held Isobel's hand as I turned back toward the gates under the stairs. As expected, they were locked, but Martin soon had them open.

'Down here,' I instructed.

I led them to the tapestry, pulling it aside to find the clock-tower door open. Perhaps we were expected. It didn't really matter as long as we put an end to this mystery as soon as possible, bringing the culprit out of the woodwork.

'Who do you remember from your childhood, Isobel?' I asked.

'Why?'

'Well, if anyone you recall stands out as unusual, it could help us.'

'Oh,' she said. 'Must we go down here? Perhaps we

should leave and go to find some help …'

'It's my experience that the local constabulary of any area aren't very good at dealing with supernatural activity,' Martin said. 'You don't know it, but we are the best help you could have.'

Isobel clung to him but bravely followed as I passed through the doorway and down the five steps.

The torches were lit in the clock tower.

'I've never been down here,' Isobel said. 'I've just realised, you mentioned a clock tower … but our house doesn't have a clock tower …'

I paused at the doorway. 'Vincenzio was maintaining the machinery. He said your father had a passion for clockwork.'

Isobel shook her head. 'No, he didn't. Just his dungeon. Just that role-playing and the wax figures. But now … I'm not even sure about that.'

'You've been duped by someone – hypnotised, maybe – into believing all that you see and are told is real. It's my suspicion that some drugging is involved. Something in the food and drink to make you more susceptible to the brainwashing. I've come across that before.[3]'

'Let's find out what's going on here,' said Martin. He pushed past me and opened the door to the tower room.

---

[3] See *Kat of Green Tentacles*.

# 14

I woke in total darkness.

My cheek was resting on a slab of icy, damp stone. My body was chilled, hands and arms numb and tingling. I turned from my side onto my back and gazed upwards – there was only a suffocating emptiness around me.

I rubbed my arms, forcing the blood to start re-circulating. My fingers hurt with the numbing cold. I rubbed them together until they started to feel more alive. Then I pulled myself up into a sitting position. It was a relief to not have the cold ground on my back.

Where was I? My head was foggy. And as I pressed my hand to my forehead, something warm and sticky was drying there. I sniffed my fingers but knew already that my blood had been seeping out from a head wound. I ran my fingers lightly over my skull and discovered that the damage was at the back of my head – the blood had dripped forward and was congealing in my hair.

Had I fallen? Or had I been hit? And if the latter was the case, by whom?

More importantly, who was *I*?

I wiped the sticky mess from my fingers onto the skirt of the dress I was wearing. The fabric was light and flowing. I had a small flash of memory of seeing myself in a mirror wearing this dress. If my recollection was correct, I had dark hair and blue eyes, and the dress was purple.

Funeral colours.

I paused in my thoughts about the dress and considered what I meant by 'funeral colours'. But it seemed apt even to my addled mind, so I pushed the doubt in myself aside.

I reached a hand out to the left side of me and met only with air. I did the same on the right and found nothing. There must be sides to this room: there had to be a doorway too. I shuffled left on instinct, hands reaching out to the floor ahead to ensure that there was something under me before I moved. Soon I felt a hard surface in front of me. It was smooth and felt nothing like the flagstones I had been lying on. It was of some kind of metal.

*Curious.*

I pressed my head against the wall. It would be my security in this room of uncertainty. All I had to do was walk along and around it until I found a door.

There was logic to this thought, at least. If I was a prisoner, then I might learn who my captors were and why I was here. If I was somehow trapped by accident, then I could call for help. Either way, I hoped that someone would find me if I made enough noise, and then I might recall who I was and why I was there.

I climbed to my feet and pressed my back against the wall. Then I stretched my hand upwards to see if I could feel anything above. My hand met with thin air: the ceiling was higher up than I could reach.

I became aware of the dress floating around my legs. The front had been ripped away to the knees, and my lower legs were bare. I felt insecure, but it made moving easier, and I had a recollection of tearing the front away myself.

I edged left, back against the wall. My hand searched the wall ahead before I moved, and my right foot tested the ground before I took a step.

I followed the shape of the room, expecting at any moment that I would come to a corner, but the wall curved and continued on until I realised that I had traversed all of the space. The room was not square, rectangular, or any other shape that might be deemed normal. If I had indeed gone around the entire circumference, then it confirmed to me that there was no door either. My prison, it appeared, was round. Had I somehow fallen down a well, knocking my head on the way?

I looked upwards, squinting for any sign of light. But there was not the faintest trace anywhere. If I had been in a well, even if it was night-time, some light would have shown the shape of the rim above.

Where was I?

Then the sound started: a sharp scraping noise, a stir of air above. I had the distinct impression that something was moving, some kind of machinery, far above my head.

What was this? The whoosh of air cleared my lungs, sharpened my mind, and I refocused on the puzzle of where I might be. Then the wall behind me shifted, twisted. I stepped away, moving toward the centre of the space, feeling insecure as air swirled around me not just from the thing that moved above my head but from the twisting now of the circular walls. The sound echoed around the space, and suddenly I could see. Edges and shapes flashed into my vision. It was not 'sight' in any traditional sense, but it was enough for me to make sense of my environment.

There was a complexity of machinery, though this flashing imagery hung before my eyes unexplained.

'What's happening?' I called.

My voice echoed off the walls, and images of greyish light sparked in the air, allowing me to 'see' more of my surroundings.

I had thought my prison was some form of horrific oubliette or deep well, but now I could see it was more than that. The walls were definitely moving. Gone was the smooth metal. Now large cogs and wheels turned on either side of me. I was rooted to the spot for fear of becoming entangled in them.

'Someone help me!' I called again.

Then I remembered. I could see whenever I spoke. I had echo-location vision. *Just like a bat.* I knew this, but couldn't recall how or why. And the movement of the machinery had sparked that skill, giving me my first glimpse of my prison.

I felt the whoosh of air moving above me again, and I glanced upwards just in time to see something flashing across the space. On instinct, I whistled, and the thing became clearer. It was a huge pendulum, the movement of which drove a large clock, higher up and just out of range of my vision. I heard the sound now. The tick, tick, tick of the clock above the grind and screech of the hellish mechanism.

The walls spun faster around me. I began to feel sick and dizzy with the movement.

'Stop it! Please!' I shouted.

I was frightened now, and sure that any moment I would empty the contents of my stomach onto the ground of this perpetually spinning room.

A loud creak of what sounded like grinding cogs echoed above my head, and I felt a chill running down my spine as something else swished above my head. I glanced up. Sound echoed around me, and I could make out the shape of a pair of metal tracks running down the walls and ending just above my head. The pendulum was descending by increments as it rocked from side to side, even as the walls turned. One moment it crossed at a certain angle, another it randomly changed course, twisting onto a different path. Another groan and creak and I could make out the wheels that carried the pendulum down the tracks.

Then I realised that the pendulum's base was not the usual type of spherical weight that helped a clock keep perfect time. No, this was flat and angled; and as the sound of the cogs and gears continued to echo around me, I saw the bevelled lower edge that was now barely a few feet above my head.

It was like a scythe, gradually descending toward me on its tracks; and the way it twisted and turned, there was no way I could anticipate in what direction the hissing blade would slice next.

I crouched down on my haunches as the wheels dropped lower and the moving air ruffled my already tousled hair.

How long did I have? Who had put me here? Why did they want to kill me?

And then I remembered.

Yes, Isobel and Martin had been with me. My memory returned in one sudden rush that made my head spin.

Martin had gone first into the tower room and I had been left behind. As I had started to follow, something had hit me from behind. I had called out and tumbled forward …

That was the last thing I could recall before waking up alone in this awful place.

The clock might not have been designed as a torture device, but it had certainly become one now. Whoever had put me inside this pit of machinery had known that the pendulum would work its way down.

The clock ticked onwards, and the wheels moved another notch further down the tracks.

Abruptly, and with a clash of screaming gears, the walls stopped spinning. I realised that the pendulum was no longer being worked by the mechanism, but was being propelled by its own momentum. The wheels dropped a further increment down the tracks. I crouched low: the pendulum was barely two feet above my head.

I looked at the stone floor, and my echo-location showed me crossing score marks all over it … Even if I lay down flat, the blade would still reach me. The pendulum would sweep across me during its twisting and turning, and there was no way I could survive. I would be cut to pieces.

There was no way out.

Tick.

Tick.

Now that the infernal machinery had stopped, I was seeing next to no flashes of my predicament. I whistled once more as the wheels clicked forward another notch and the blade dropped farther down.

Tick.

I was on all fours now, directly beneath the moving blade. It swept over my hair, and a loose strand was caught in the updraft, nicked and cut; with the final echo of sound around me, I saw the severed strand fall. The blade was obviously very sharp. Knife-edge sharp.

Tick.

Tick.

# 15

I really was in a pit of despair. There was no hope; no help was coming, and I had no way of getting out of the mechanical oubliette.

An unbidden memory came back to me.

I was in our dining-room back in New York. Mother had entered carrying a book she had found in Grandpapa's library. A small, hardback tome.

I asked her what it was, and she explained that it was called *The Gift: A Christmas and New Year's Present for 1843*. She mentioned that it contained a tale of terror she had read the night before. Something by a man with the unusual name of Poe. When I asked what the tale was about, she would say only that it was a horror story about the Spanish Inquisition, and involved the inventive use of a pendulum as an instrument of torture …

Well, that seemed to fit my predicament quite neatly … Perhaps whoever had seen fit to create this hellish clocktower had read the same story.

Then it occurred to me that there might be a way out: what if I was able to jam something in the tracks, stopping the wheels from making that final drop? The pendulum would still swing, but it wouldn't reach me. It might be all

I needed to allow time for Pepper to find me. For surely he was looking for me?

I thought for a moment: what could I use to block the tracks?

My weapons were gone, my feet bare. I had no hard objects at all on me that I could use to stop that thing from dropping lower.

Thinking hard, I remembered that the ground was paved with stone flags. I began to claw at them. If I could only dislodge one of the flags, then I could wedge it into the mechanism. My fingers dug into the cracks and dragged at the dirt between. My echo-location vision gave me a view of the flag beneath me. My luck was in; it was loose and already broken on one corner. Perhaps it had been damaged the last time the pendulum had run across it? I shuddered.

I tugged and pulled at the corner of the flag using all of my strength. The broken piece came away in my hand. I grasped it: a sharp edge dug into my palm, but I had to hold on until the right moment.

Waiting until the pendulum passed above me and scythed away, I reached up to the last notch on one of the tracks and slammed the stone into it, dropping back to the floor immediately afterwards.

The mechanism screamed. It reminded me of the night when Vincenzio had been oiling it. And maybe the forces behind my capture had been influencing him to prepare the machine for just this purpose – although I didn't want to think that they had been quite so calculating in their intended removal of me. It is easy to become paranoid when you find your life on the line. If I had been tied down to a train track with a locomotive rushing toward me, I could not have been any more scared than I was at that moment.

The pendulum's tilt and twist faltered. My hands reached down and found the broken corner of the side of the heavy flag. I pulled and tugged until the whole thing came free. Then I spun around onto my back, lifting the flag up before me, even as the small piece, wedged into the track above, groaned and split with the effort of holding back the heavy machinery.

I knew it wasn't going to last for long, but hoped at least to protect my face and chest from the blade by deflecting it with the stone flag. Then, the track gave and the stone shard was pushed downwards into the corner of the final notch. I waited a moment, half expecting the blade to crash down onto the flag, but nothing happened.

There was silence, and the darkness rushed in and around me once more.

I whistled, looking around the edge of the stone. It was good news: the jammed track had thrown the pendulum off kilter, and now it was moving only one way, which meant I could pull myself up and out of its path.

I turned the flag on its side and placed it under the blocked track. If the small corner piece of stone gave, then the flag itself might still hold back the pendulum.

I stood. Leaning on the smooth wall, I breathed deeply, trying to calm my ragged breath, as the pendulum jerked unevenly from one side of the space opposite me to the other. Pressed against the curving wall, I had a brief moment of respite. But when the mechanism groaned once more, I guessed that moment would soon end. By then I had realised that the only truly safe place to be was above the pendulum.

I turned and looked up, but kept myself pressed against the wall as much as possible. I whistled. Sound burst over the walls, giving me the vision I needed. There was a metal bar buried into the wall above. If I could jump high enough, I could use it as leverage. I whistled again. Above the bar, I could also see the workings of the clock and the pendulum. What I really needed to do was stop the clock from working altogether. Then the pendulum should fall still.

The pendulum jerked and turned, fighting against the blockage on the track. I waited for it to swing away, then I stepped back and leapt upwards, catching hold of the bar above. The blockage was crumbling, and it dropped with a clatter to the stone floor.

The pendulum returned to its true pattern. The blade swished below me, right where I had been standing. The wheeled mechanism in the wall knocked the wedged stone flag clear. And then the pendulum was swinging and twisting and turning below me.

But now I was out of its way.

I pulled myself up on the bar, hoping it would hold my weight. Whistling again, I saw now that I could use the notches in the track as footholds, and I swung myself left until I reached one. Holding onto the bar, I climbed up the mechanical pit. Another whistle revealed another bar above my head, just within reach, and I began to pull myself up, one bar at a time, until I reached a foot-wide ledge around the top of the pit.

There was a mechanical fan spinning and clattering above my head, which explained where the current of air had come from. I sat on the ledge and looked up at it. Was that my only way out?

I checked all of the sides of the pit, and then I noticed opposite me a metal panel that jutted out slightly farther than the rest.

The ledge circumscribed the whole of the rim, and I slid along it with the agility and balance of a cat, until I was close to the panel.

I ran my fingers carefully over the ledge and felt the protruding edge of the panel near my legs. I hadn't been mistaken. It was some form of access point, and it hadn't been properly closed and secured.

I prised the thing open with my now sore fingers. It dropped downwards on hinges, to reveal an opening beyond. I speculated on the possibility of my assailant having dragged me into the pit this way, and dropped me down to the bottom. Such a fall would probably have killed any normal human, but I wasn't completely normal since being bitten by vampires and then cured by my cat Holly. Whatever vampire/cat hybrid I had become since, it gave me great agility, and I healed quickly, making me harder to kill than if I had been merely human. Maybe I also had nine lives …

I slid into the narrow opening and crawled along a short tunnel.

Abruptly there was no floor ahead of me. My hand waved in thin air for a moment before I realised that there was a ladder going down.

I took a moment to breathe. Had I done it? Had I not only avoided being cut to ribbons by the strange pendulum blade, but also found a way out of the pit?

I shimmied my way around and then paused at the top of the ladder. Where did this lead? I reflected that my assailant was certainly strong, and inventive. Their attempt to kill me had been brutal and cruel, designed to cause me the maximum amount of fear and pain. Whoever they were, there would be payback, but I had to be cautious and make sure that there wasn't another trap waiting for me below.

I took a careful step down, with the lightest tread I could. Then another, and another. Before long, I had reached the bottom of the ladder without incident.

I realised that I was now standing on the platform that I had seen from below when we had found Vincenzio here the night before. It was gave me a very high vantage point, and as I glanced down, I saw that the interior of the tower was just as I had remembered it.

Now that I was out of danger, I began to think back over all of the strange things that had occurred over the last few days. It was obvious that we had all been subjected to some form of glamour. The castle of Vincenzio Precio did not exist. I now began to wonder about Precio himself. He, like his sister Isobel, appeared to be an actor playing a part for our benefit.

I began to worry about what had happened to Martin. If I had ended up in the pit with a dangerous pendulum, then what had become of him? Just as importantly, where was Pepper? Was he still trapped in that peculiar ballroom with Precio, Beth and Carlos?

It occurred to me that Nicolas hadn't been present in that little scenario. So, who was he, and could he be behind this whole thing?

I looked around the platform, trying to remember why I had even wanted to come back to the clock tower. Ah yes! Of course! The clock tower was the only thing that had remained the same throughout, wasn't it? And the strange stone circles had seemed to be sending energy to it.

There was a hatch in the platform, leading onto the wooden stairs that zigzagged across the side of the tower. I needed to get down and away from here. I had to find Pepper and Martin as soon as possible, because I needed my friends to help me solve this puzzle and I wanted to make sure they were both all right.

I reached the hatch but paused. Looking back at the workings of the clock, I recalled how Vincenzio had been so enthused about it. The cogs and workings ticked and clicked beside the hatch. This clock had nearly killed me. I was angry about that and wanted to take some form of revenge; but to harbour resentment toward an inanimate mechanism would be ridiculous.

I shook my head. There would be time later to make sure that no-one else was put into the pit, but for now I had to find Pepper and Martin.

I hurried down the stairs.

# 16

The castle was in a state of flux. One moment it was fully realised, another it was back to being a rock cavern – and at those times the temperature plummeted and I found myself shivering in the thin dress.

I reached the top of the castle steps leading up to the landing just before they transformed to roughly-carved indents in the rock. Once there, I looked toward the wing where Pepper and I had shared a room. If my calculation was correct, my carpetbag, and the remains of my weapons, should still be in the room. All I had to do was wait until the castle reappeared once more, then I should be able to enter the room, find my equipment and change out of this damned dress and back into some breeches. Fighting the forces of evil in a sheer bit of fabric wasn't ideal, after all; and I had to find Pepper and Martin and try to get us all safely out of this madness.

I ran down the stone passageway ahead of me, searching the alcoves that I knew represented bedrooms in the castle. It made me fully aware of how we had indeed been duped by a magical trickster, who had been able to manipulate reality to his advantage.

I saw the door to our room shimmer back into place

and reached for the handle.

Paranoia overwhelmed me again, and I hesitated. Did my enemy know yet that I had escaped his clockwork pit? Could this be another trap?

I took a breath and opened the door.

Inside I found the room filled with furniture, and the fire blazing in the hearth.

Pepper was asleep in the bed; his face turned toward the door was illuminated by the glow from the fire. I hurried to his side and gently placed my hand on his shoulder.

'Pepper?' I said. 'Wake up. Thank goodness I found you.'

He remained still and unmoving, and I shook him a little. In response, he gave a low groan.

'What's the matter, darling?' he asked.

I was a little shocked by him calling me 'darling', but then recalled that we had both been taken in by the situation earlier and had started to become romantically inclined again. I tried to tell myself that it had to have been a spell; but deep down, in my heart, I knew that wasn't the case. Pepper had always had these feelings for me. I'd known it all along. And I, despite my frequent denials, felt the same about him.

'Pepper ...' I said softly. 'Please wake. Things aren't what they seem here. Don't you remember?'

He turned onto his back and rubbed his eyes. 'Kat?'

'Yes. It's me. We need to talk, before the castle changes back into rock again.'

'Who is there, darling?' said a voice, and then I realised that Pepper was not alone in the bed.

I took a step back, shocked. I hadn't seen her in the shadow of his body, curled so closely into him. Her hand now slid around his waist and I noticed that she was wearing my ring.

I looked down at my hand. The ring was no longer there!

The woman pulled herself up. She had dark hair, was slender. She was even wearing one of my nightgowns!

Then she pushed back the hair from her face and I found myself looking into the eyes of my mirror image.

'What is this?' I gasped.

I fell back, crashing into the doorframe, unable to say any more as the awful changeling stepped from the bed and walked toward me.

'Good heavens, I would never be dressed like that,' the creature said. Her voice was scathing.

I glanced down at my clothing. Saw the torn, flimsy gown and my bare legs, and realised the dishevelled state I must be in. And she – she was perfect, beautiful in the way I wasn't. She appeared soft and voluptuous. Even the bed-tousled hair shook out into smooth and perfect waves that framed her face.

Yes, she was me; but she was the me I might have been if I hadn't discovered the reality of the Darkness. She was the me who had never faced zombies, fought demons or taken down an ancient evil from another dimension.

I looked at Pepper, saw the confusion and love in his eyes as his gaze passed from one to the other of us, and I wanted to run away. Surely this other version of me was what he deserved – not the real me with my paranoia and suspicion! He should not have to be content with a woman who knew she could never settle down to anything as mundane as marriage and children, unless she knew that the world was free of supernatural evil.

'Who are you?' he said now, and I buried my face in my hands, afraid to see the rejection in his. Of course he would choose the perfect creature that had lain beside him. Why wouldn't he?

'Kat? Kat?' he said. 'What the hell was that thing?'

I looked up as I realised he was actually addressing me. He was out of bed now, and he stood before me.

'You *recognised* me?' I said, looking around. The other me was gone now.

'Of course I did. That pathetic shadow wasn't a patch on you.'

'She was … perfect,' I said. 'Wasn't she?'

'No,' Pepper said. 'You're perfect. She wasn't even as solid as your reflection in a pool.'

I fell into his arms and he held me. I was shaking. The night had brought too much strangeness and confusion. I poured out the story of what had happened.

He pulled me down onto the edge of the bed, pressing my head against his shoulder. I was weak, and not my usual self. Where was the strong Kat Lightfoot? Maybe I *was* the changeling after all?

'Something is playing with us,' he concluded. 'And I don't recall any of the events you've recounted. All I remember is going to sleep tonight. Nothing more.'

'Then everything was staged for my benefit,' I said.

'Perhaps. Or maybe you had a nightmare. But that wouldn't explain the other creature that took your place beside me. Look, I think we had both better go and investigate. Try and get something tangible we can hold onto, and above all find Martin and make sure he and Isobel are okay.'

'I agree,' I said. 'But first I need to change.'

I went to my trunk and found all of my things back in there: my breeches, my shirt, my boots; even my weapons. I took them all out and went behind the screen. As I pulled away the dress, something dropped to the floor at my feet. I looked down. It was the ring that Pepper had given me.

It appeared that the changeling could look like me but not hold onto my possessions when the spell was broken.

When I was dressed and armed, Pepper and I left the room – this time hand in hand.

'I'm not letting you out of my sight,' I said.

'Quite right, too,' he smiled, and raised his eyebrow in that familiar quirky way he had when he was trying to be light-hearted but was really deeply troubled.

I smiled back, and some of the tension went from his brow. He looked happy, despite our circumstances, and I knew why: he had noticed the change in me. I had never shown any fear or weakness in front of him before, but the thought that I had almost lost him had been worse than the near-death experience of the mechanical pit and the pendulum.

I was both weak and strong in my new mindset. If we got out of this alive, things were going to change: I couldn't keep Pepper dangling anymore.

I shook my head, and then mentally chastised myself for not concentrating on the task in hand. If we were going to resolve this mystery, then I had to stop thinking about my feelings for Pepper and instead focus on the danger we were in.

With my free hand, I withdrew my pistol from its holster in my weapons belt and pointed it ahead of us.

'Are you expecting an attack?' Pepper asked.

'I don't know. But someone did leave me for dead tonight.'

Pepper nodded. He also had a gun in his hand, and I hadn't noticed him removing it from its holster while I had been deep in thought. Sloppy. I forced my mind to the present.

The corridor outside of our room had changed. It now had tapestried walls on one side and rock face on the other, proving that I hadn't imagined the whole thing after all.

'Curious,' murmured Pepper. 'It would take a lot of magic to sustain a delusion of this magnitude. Hence, I think, why it is slipping. Maybe our illusionist believes us all to be soundly asleep right now and is resting?'

'You could be right.'

At the end of the corridor, the staircase landing no longer had a railing. There was a sheer drop down into the cavern that was the former reception room.

'That way should lead to Martin's room,' I said.

'It does,' said Pepper.

We followed a rock-walled corridor and came to the place where Martin's room had been.

'Wait,' I said. 'He was with me. Down in the clock tower, with Isobel. Why would he now be in bed?'

'You thought I had left our room with you too. What if they also were merely phantoms?'

When we opened the door to Martin's room, however, all we found was a hollow cave. There was no sign of him, though his possessions remained scattered over the rock floor.

'Where to now?' I said.

'I think it's time we saw what was beyond the kitchen area.'

Pepper was right: it would be a good place to start. We still hadn't gotten beyond that point in the castle structure, and it hadn't occurred to me to look there when the place had reverted to a rock cave.

I began to wish that I had put on my Remington 51 with the automatic cartridge backpack. There were thousands of bullets in the cartridge, all filled with diamond shards. The forces of evil were often allergic to diamonds, and it made a powerful weapon.

But I did have my diamond blade back in its holster inside my boot, and it pressed against my ankle. This gave me some reassurance. The laser gun in my hand was pretty lethal too. Plus, Pepper was well-armed. Nothing could take us by surprise again. Could it? I pushed back the thought that this demon's magic had already stripped me of my weapons once that evening and could easily do so again.

I made my way down the rock staircase, keeping my back against the wall and feet away from the slippery and treacherous edge. Pepper followed. At the bottom, we turned in the direction of the dining-room and, hand in hand, walked toward the kitchen.

We reached an archway. Beyond was a long tunnel leading off into darkness.

Pepper swapped places with me and took over the lead, bowing his head slightly to pass through the low and narrow arch and into the tunnel. I followed, holding onto his belt now instead of his hand, though it felt awkward to be clinging onto him all of the time.

Pepper rounded a corner and came to a stop.

I looked up and saw we were outside again. This time, we had emerged into the clearing in the middle of the circle of stones.

A pool now lay in the centre of the circle, and it was surrounded by a beautiful fairy glen, of which the stones were a part.

I let go of Pepper's belt and came around him.

'It's no use, there's nothing here and we are being duped into seeing things again,' I murmured.

'No. I don't think so. I think we are seeing the real

thing,' Pepper said. 'Look.'

At the other side of the pool was a humped hill, on which were scattered millions of red petals. In the centre lay a woman with long, flowing, dark blonde hair that draped over the edge of a makeshift bed.

'Fae,' I said.

We stepped forward, expecting the woman to awake, but she lay asleep. Around her, blossoms grew and spread, covering the stone circle.

As we drew near, another figure raised its head. And then I recognised Carlos.

The man was in a terrible state, worse still than I had seen him the day before. He had grown thin and his clothing was in rags.

'Help me,' he pleaded. 'We have to get away while she sleeps. It's the only way.'

'Come away,' I said.

Then he raised his ankle and I saw a chain of daisies wrapped around it.

'I can't leave,' he groaned.

I moved forward, caught hold of the chain and tugged. Despite its delicate appearance, it wouldn't break. So, on impulse, I retrieved my knife from my boot and slashed at the green vine between two of the daisies. The powerful silver and diamond-shard blade worked: the daisy-chain fell away, rotting rapidly until it turned to dust.

Carlos took my hand, and I pulled him away from the creature's nest.

'We have to leave before she wakes,' he said. 'Once she regains her strength, she'll bespell us all and we'll never escape.'

'Who is she?' I said.

'She's a Xana,' he said. 'The worst kind of nymph.

They bespell men and use them up, sucking the life from them.'

'She's been draining you?' Pepper said. 'How?'

'Not me,' said Carlos. 'I wouldn't give in to her. I did not take the food and drink when I realised what she was.'

'I knew it!' I said. 'We've been drugged to make us more susceptible …'

'Please,' Carlos begged, 'let us leave here now! I'll take my chances in the desert outside rather than spend another night here.'

I'm no fool, and neither is Pepper, so we began to back away from the Xana.

'We can't leave without Martin and Isobel,' I said. 'And I suspect that Dr Brewster and Vincenzio are around here somewhere too.'

The woman on the petals began to stir just as we reached the tunnel leading back into the cave. Carlos panicked and ran on ahead, re-entering the cave.

Then the creature sat up and looked straight at me.

'You!' I said.

It was Isobel.

She swung her legs over the edge of her flower-covered bed and stood up.

The petals withered, the hump and pool waned and disappeared, and then we were in the centre of the maze, and moonlight was reflecting from the sundial.

Isobel drew herself up to her full height, and we saw that she was far taller than she had appeared previously. I glanced behind me and noted that Carlos had gone. I hoped he had reached far enough away to escape the evil clutches of this creature.

'Where is Martin?' Pepper demanded.

There was an ethereal glow around Isobel now, and I

became aware of a change in Pepper. I heard music. It was the same melody that had compelled me through the underground glen and into the ballroom, but this time it had no affect on me. Pepper, though, began to move forward as if answering the magical call.

I reached out my hand to pull him back. The diamond-shard and silver knife scratched his skin. He yelped and then looked at me in surprise.

'I'm sorry!' I said. I couldn't believe that I had done such an amateurism thing as to forget that I had a weapon in my hand before reaching for him.

'You saved me!' he gasped. 'She … I was *compelled!*'

I pulled Pepper close to my side.

'Wrap your arm around my waist and don't let go,' I said.

Pepper did as I said, and I looked once more at Isobel.

'Where is Martin?' I asked.

Isobel laughed. 'He belongs to me. But I'm feeling generous this evening, so take your man and that pathetic driver and I'll let you leave.'

'Not without Martin,' I said.

'Then you will all remain until I've fed enough,' she said.

'Enough for what?' asked Pepper.

Isobel smiled. She was stunning, but her expression wasn't pretty. I could see that this Xana was not fae. It was obvious once you knew what to look for. The fae could be mischievous, but they were not on the whole evil. This Xana was a demon. I just did not know what type, or how to destroy her. Yet.

'How did you escape my pit?' she asked me. 'And *you*, my changeling?' she said to Pepper.

'You underestimated both of us,' Pepper said. 'And how we feel about each other.'

'Not *your* emotions,' she said. 'I knew you loved her; it was obvious.'

'But you didn't realise that Pepper would see through the façade of your … changeling. He would never fail to recognise the real me.'

'That may be so,' she said. 'But what about you?'

I didn't have an opportunity to ask her what she meant, for suddenly I found Pepper was no longer at my side. Instead I was surrounded by mirrors.

The mirrors, however, did not reflect my image: they all showed Pepper, but each of them in a slightly different stance. Then the figures all stepped from the mirrors and began to walk around me in a circle.

'It's me. I'm the real Pepper,' said the first one.

'Don't let her trick you, Kat, I'm Pepper,' said another.

I was overwhelmed as they all surrounded me. All of them claimed to be my best friend in the whole world, and I couldn't tell them apart.

Self-doubt can bring the strongest conviction to its knees. I regarded each of the Peppers in turn, unsure which was the real one, and it made me consider that I had no feelings at all. How could I have known him for so long, yet not recognise him among these changelings, as easily as he had recognised me?

'Not fair!' said a voice, and one of the Peppers approached me. 'It's not your fault,' he said. 'I had only one to compare you with.'

'Very well,' said Isobel.

All but two Peppers disappeared, and the one who had spoken was one of those that remained.

I looked from one to the other, but thought it obvious that the one who had spoken must be genuine, and so I moved toward him. Then I saw something in the face of the other Pepper that made me realise how wrong I was.

I saw genuine hurt in his eyes, and so I reached for him and called his name, just as he had done with me.

The other creature vanished.

Isobel swayed on her feet and then tumbled to the ground.

# 17

We stood over the creature, looking down at her withered and frail frame. It was clear that Isobel's power had been exhausted by her attempts to confuse and control us.

'I only wanted to become free,' she said.

'Free from what?' I asked.

Her eyes fell behind me, and I turned to see the clock tower, tall and imposing against the moonlit sky.

'Five hundred years I had been trapped. And then, Vincenzio found me.'

Her story unfolded before us. A Xana, or river nymph, she was not evil but seductive. Her power had been used to fuel the clock that some evil creature had built into the rock. She had slept in the circle of stones: it had been her prison. Her heartbeat had been the tick of the clock: it had propelled the pendulum.

'How can I believe anything you say?' I asked. 'And if this is all true, then what did Vincenzio do to free you?'

'He came into my circle,' Isobel said. 'He gave me his adoration. and it fed me. Then I was free to move beyond the circle. But not far.'

'And so you took on the image of his sister?' Pepper said. 'And became part of his life.'

Isobel laughed, but it was weak. 'He has no sister, but I was happy to fulfil the role. I built this castle for him. Then, Bethany … became suspicious. I had to remove her from the equation. I had to possess Vincenzio fully, or I would never become completely free.'

'*You* killed Beth?' I asked.

'Perhaps you'd like to see what happened to her?' Isobel said.

Another of the mirrors appeared before us, and as I looked into it, it began to reveal the movements of Bethany Precio in her final hours. I could see and hear everything, even her thoughts. I reached for Pepper's hand as we stood before the mirror, voyeurs, helpless to intervene in the events that unfolded before us.

We saw Bethany Precio in her bedroom alone, heard her tortured thoughts and doubts. Then we watched as she made her way downstairs to the dungeon.

When she entered the dungeon, she became even more afraid. Turning to leave, she found herself locked in.

She was trapped. Trapped in a pit of despair. And down below there was someone in a black robe, looking for all the world like one of those fearful Inquisitors from her husband's ancestral past.

Her heart beat faster as she looked down and the robed spectre looked up. Then Bethany screamed. It was the same sound we had heard every night since we had arrived here. The shrill, desperate call of an animal caught in a trap.

But the robed figure did not move, and Bethany saw someone else now: a woman. The woman emerged from the shadows and stared up at her, just as the robed figure did.

Beth could see who it was now. It was Vincenzio's sister, newly arrived from Madrid. How had she forgotten that Isobel was in the castle?

'Isobel!' she said. 'What is going on here?'

'He's mine,' Isobel replied, and then she embraced the robed figure, pushing back the black cowl to reveal Vincenzio.

The music took up again, and Isobel's lips clamped against Vincenzio's. Beth cried out!

But it was as though Vincenzio was unaware of her presence.

'You're not his sister!' Beth said.

'No. Vincenzio has no sister,' Isobel laughed. 'He's mine. My slave. There is nothing you can do.'

Beth picked up the front of her nightgown and hurried down the steps.

'Vinni!' she called. 'Come back to me!'

Vincenzio turned his eyes toward Beth, and for a moment she saw the pain and fear in them. Then Isobel touched him, and he turned his eyes back to her. Completely bespelled.

'You bitch!' Beth said, and she raised her hand to strike Isobel.

'Go to the ball …' Isobel said.

Beth found herself turning away. She danced back up the steps.

A moment later, a body lay at the foot of the steps by Vincenzio's feet.

'Look, brother,' said Isobel. 'Your prank has frightened Beth to death.'

Vincenzio snapped out of his trance and then fell to his knees before the body. He began to weep.

'It's all my fault!'

The mirror disappeared, and I found myself facing Isobel. Blue circles were under her eyes. Her strength ebbed and flowed with moments of brilliance that she almost couldn't stop herself from using. I realised that this was beyond her control. While we remained awake and alert, she was forced to try to take control of us.

'So you *did* kill Beth?' Pepper said. He held my hand tight.

'She is in the ballroom,' I said. 'I saw her.'

'Yes,' Isobel confirmed. 'Not dead, but under my spell. She will dance and dance until I break free.'

'But what about the body Vincenzio saw?' I asked.

'An illusion,' Isobel said.

'So Vincenzio is in your ballroom too?' Pepper said.

'Yes,' Isobel confirmed.

We continued to fire questions at her. She was compelled to answer, even though I was unsure if what she said or showed us was true.

'Who captured you?' I asked. 'And why?'

The mirror was before us again. It appeared that Isobel couldn't stop herself from showing us the past; and this was the way it had unfolded for her.

We saw this time a young man wearing medieval hose and doublet. He had ridden his horse up to the rock. An early adventurer, perhaps.

Isobel swam in the pool, but was aware of the new arrival. The first male to pass this way in some time.

'Nymph!' he called.

Isobel had hidden herself behind one of the stones, but the man knew she was there. He had power, equal to her own, and even as she sang her siren song of seduction, he weaved his magic around her, capturing her within the stones.

'He knew fae magic, but was not from the faery folk,' Isobel said. 'And soon the clock formed within the rock. He cut a strand of my hair and weaved it into the workings.

'I begged him to tell me who he was, but never learned the truth.'

'You are a victim,' I said. 'But of someone you would have destroyed with your power, given half a chance. It is difficult have sympathy for you.'

'Most men left me with only a few years of their life taken,' she said. 'I did not kill. Then.'

'Why do you need to drain the lives of Vincenzio and Martin?' asked Pepper.

'When Martin arrived I no longer needed Vincenzio,' she said.

'Why?' asked Pepper.

'His will is strong. Stronger than anyone's I've ever come across.'

'Where *is* Martin?' I asked.

Isobel shook her head. 'You've exhausted me.'

'Where is he?' I pursued.

From inside the cave, even when it was the castle, I had not heard the clock marking any hour, but now it began to chime.

Pepper's hand was in mine, and it was just as well, for the Xana had not finished with us yet.

Despite her dwindling strength, the world around us changed again.


We were in each other's arms, dancing around a central table that was heaving with food. My stomach growled: my body was weak with hunger and thirst.

'We mustn't eat,' Pepper said. 'Or we'll be lost.'

I saw Martin in Isobel's arms; they danced, always on the other side of the table from us. I fought against the pull of the music. And Pepper tried to help, but it was like swimming against a strong current: every time we thought we were gaining on them, something pulled us back.

Isobel led Martin from the dance floor. We danced past: the music became wild and fast. My feet knew all of the moves, even though I had never been one for this sort of dance.

I began to worry about Pepper's leg, and how his old war wound would hold up to this onslaught. Our steps faltered. Then the dance took us again. We had had, for a fraction of a second, some control, which made me believe that there had to be a way out of this.

Vincenzio passed us with Beth in his arms. He was happy to be with his wife, but they were both still under the control of Isobel, as was Edward Brewster as he danced with a young girl. Who was she? A servant who had been captured along with others?

'We have to get away,' I yelled over the music.

'I know,' said Pepper.

I caught sight of Isobel. She held Martin's face between her hands and pulled him toward her, lips puckered for a kiss.

'How's your leg?' I asked Pepper.

'It hurts,' he said.

I was afraid for him, and once more our dancing stopped for the merest second.

'That's it,' I said. 'It's my emotions ...'

'What is?'

'I'm worried about you,' I said. 'I can't let you be hurt.'

Pepper stopped dancing, and even though my feet tried to continue, I found I could force them to be still now. I just had to keep my feelings for Pepper foremost in my mind.

'Walk,' he said.

He walked away from the dance floor and toward

Martin and Isobel.

Martin was looking into the Xana's eyes with such love and trust that I hated what I was about to do.

At some point I had returned my dagger to its holster in my boot. I didn't recall when or how, but I could feel it there, and now bent to pull it free.

I reached out with the dagger, quickly and lightly scratching Martin across the back of one hand.

He yelped, and his arms dropped from Isobel's waist.

She turned to me then, and in her fury her mask dropped.

I saw what she really was. Her true face. Not some beautiful water nymph, guilty of little more than trying to maintain her survival. No, she was a cold and deceitful demon. Though the face was still that of Isobel, I could now see the marks of her evil nature in the boils and scars that marred her former beauty. One thing we had learned over the years was that evil deeds did indeed show on the face of a demon – that is, when you saw its *true* face.

'My god …' said Martin as he saw it too. 'Who … what … are you?'

The room went suddenly quiet. The musicians and dancers disappeared – as did the tempting food and drink.

We were in an empty cavern now, and Isobel's world was slowly unravelling.

'Martin …' she said, stepping forward. But Martin backed away, and Pepper took his arm.

Isobel withered. Her already slender frame shrank. Her back bowed and her skin sagged as though with extreme age. She had exhausted her power trying to captivate us all, and to keep the illusion of the castle, and now she had lost her only source of energy: Martin was no longer under her spell.

The rock above us rumbled. The structure juddered, and then the walls began to close in around us. This showed that the rock had not been naturally carved out but was solid matter that she had manipulated.

'The rock.' I gasped. 'It's restructuring, and we'll all be crushed!'

The three of us hurried for the only opening ahead, and passed through into a shallow tunnel that began to collapse behind us as we ran.

'This way!' shouted Pepper above the din.

I caught hold of Martin's hand and pulled him out of the tunnel into another damp cavern.

'This one looks stable,' Pepper said. 'But we have to find our way out quickly, just in case.'

I looked around, saw the rock pool, the moss-covered earth and the impossible flowers and plant life that were now withering. I recognised the space as the one I'd found myself in earlier.

'I think I know the way,' I said.

We hurried through the cavern to another tunnel at the far end. This one was narrow to begin with and opened out as we passed through it.

'I came through here when I left our room earlier this evening,' I explained to Pepper.

'Where are we?' asked Martin as we came out onto a wider corridor.

'This,' I said, 'is where Pepper and I were sleeping. It was one of the castle wings.'

'I don't understand,' Martin said.

Pepper hurried to explain some of our exploits and findings as we hurried along. Our room was now a cavern, but in the centre was my weapons bag and trunk, as well as Pepper's trunk.

I picked up the carpetbag in case we needed any more

artillery. Then we hurried back toward the stone steps that led down into the former reception room.

'I see,' said Martin, looking down over the sheer edge.

'Be careful walking down,' I warned him. 'It's slippery and dangerous.'

We all reached the bottom though without incident.

'What about Vincenzio, Beth and Edward?' Pepper said. 'We should try to find them.'

'*Beth*?' said Martin. 'She's *alive*?'

'We have much to tell you, my friend,' said Pepper. 'But first let's get out of this place in case it closes up on us.'

We hurried out of the reception room, into the small foyer, and out through the arched opening that was the cave's only obvious entrance.

Outside there was no longer a courtyard or high walls separating us from the desert landscape. We could walk away from this and nothing could prevent us. We stood for a second looking out at the dry and desolate dunes that tumbled away to the horizon.

I turned and looked at the arch, and waited to see if anything changed. Meanwhile, Pepper filled Martin in on the rest of what we knew. Then I told him about my near-death experience in the clock tower.

Afterwards we lapsed into silence, watching the archway.

'How long do we wait?' asked Martin.

I shrugged, because I didn't have any answers for him.

'It depends how much hold the Xana has left on her power.' Pepper said. 'She might be keeping the rock at bay even now.'

'Was she telling the truth?' I said. 'About being captured and used by another demon? Her hair weaved into the workings of the clock?'

'It's hard to know,' Pepper replied. 'She is an evil being, so nothing she said can be trusted.'

I noted how quiet Martin was.

'Are you okay?' I asked.

'I don't remember anything at all that's happened over the last … few days, is it?'

'You got out! God be praised!' said a voice.

I turned my head in time to see Carlos leading his horses and carriage around the rock face.

'They were back in the stable area,' he said.

'You knew what Isobel was,' I said, remembering that he had voiced his fears to me. Had it been just yesterday? Or had more time passed since then?

'Yes *Doña* Lightfoot. The Xana is an evil creature. Spain has many of them. I did not realise at first. But when you all began to act confused, and didn't know how long we had been here … I did not know they were so powerful. They normally just seduce men, who are no worse for it afterwards.'

'How long has it been?' Martin asked.

'Eleven days,' Carlos said. 'Come, get in my carriage, and we'll leave this evil place.'

'We can't. We have to find Vincenzio and Beth,' Martin said.

'Yes, and Dr Brewster,' Pepper added. 'Or they may well be captivated once more.'

I glanced back at the archway. There had been no change. Could Vincenzio, Beth and Brewster still be inside?

'They disappeared,' I pointed out. 'We have no way of knowing where to.'

'I have an idea,' said Martin. 'I'm remembering something. I think I was inside that clock tower too, at some point.'

'Yes, you entered before I was struck down and put into the pit,' I said.

'I think, based on what you've told me, that the tower is the source of the Xana's power,' Martin continued.

'Why do you think that?' I asked.

'Well, it's obvious that she lied to you about it. To make you less concerned about the fact that the tower still remains in its entirety, while the rest of the place has reverted to its natural form.'

'And?' prompted Pepper.

'I think the stone circle is her prison. That much is the truth. It ties her to this piece of land, and it keeps her from her real source of power. After all, have you ever seen her enter the tower?'

'Martin might be right,' I said. 'As I entered the tower, someone struck me. Isobel was behind me, and she never did go inside that I saw. Even so, she somehow had the power to place me in the mechanical pit.'

'Kat,' said Martin. 'I did it. I put you in there when I was under her control. I *remember*.' He looked horrified. 'I even started the pendulum mechanism on its course to lower down. Oh my God! I can't believe she could coerce me to do that.'

'You weren't in your right mind,' Pepper said. 'None of us has been.'

He glanced over at me as though he expected me to deny his words. But everything that had happened between us now became questionable.

'So,' I said, changing the subject as quickly as possible, 'you think that she might have the others trapped in the tower?'

'It's possible,' said Martin. 'I think she will try to use them differently now though. I suspect they are still safe for the moment.'

'Use them how?' Pepper asked.

'She needs someone to destroy the circle. All it will take is one stone to be displaced.'

I thought back to my attempt at toppling one of the stones and wondered if the Xana had been manipulating me then too.

'I'm not sure they could do that. It's as though the stones grow from the land. They are rooted,' I said.

After much discussion we decided to re-enter the cave and try to get back down to the tower.

'I'd like to check out this pit properly, too,' said Martin. 'And the pendulum.'

I gave Carlos my carpetbag and sent him to wait for us beyond the boundary line of the former wall, keeping him and the horses out of harm's way, and free in the event that Isobel regained enough strength to rebuild the wall. Then the three of us entered the cave once more and made our way down to the entrance to the clock tower.

# 18

Below we found no narrow staircase leading down to the dungeon. Instead a narrow tunnel, probably created centuries earlier by running water, weaved and sloped downwards. The area that had held the tapestry hiding the entrance to the tower was now an exposed indent and cavern, but there was a sturdy-looking wooden door blocking the way to the tower: just the same as before.

We entered with caution. I was well aware of the dull ache I still had in my head from the last time I had ventured into the tower. Pepper held his gun and had given Martin one of the other weapons from his gun-belt. I carried my knife: it had helped me twice with the Xana so far, and I had begun to trust its efficacy in unveiling her to those she beguiled.

Inside, I showed the two men the way up to the clock and its workings, and led them up the ladder and along the service tunnel that opened onto the mechanical pit. Martin examined the inside of the pit from the vantage point of the hatch. The pendulum was still working its way around the bottom, and Pepper took my hand as Martin commented that if I hadn't been so resourceful, I wouldn't have been around to tell the tale.

'I suspect there would have been a very different outcome for all of us,' Pepper said. 'I would still be sleeping beside a changeling, and you, dear friend, would be the energy feast our Xana needed in order to break free.'

Martin was quiet as he took in Pepper's words. He spent several further moments examining the workings of the clock.

'It's impressive,' was all he said.

We decided to return to retrace our steps, but as we were descending the zigzagging wooden staircase that led back to the base of the tower, the whole structure was suddenly shaken by a powerful tremor.

'Hold on!' Pepper said, reaching for me as I almost lost my grip on the railing.

'What was that?' I wondered.

'I think our Xana is trying to uproot the stones. And she might actually be getting somewhere,' Martin said.

'They seemed impossible to move,' I said. 'How can she do it if it's her prison?'

'Maybe she's using the other three to help her,' Martin commented.

'We have to stop her,' Pepper said as another shockwave jarred us.

'Come on,' said Martin as he turned around and began to climb back up the staircase to the clock.

I ran up after him, taking the steps two at a time, followed by Pepper. Halfway up we had to grasp hold of the railing again as another tremor shook the tower so hard I thought the structure would collapse. Martin had reached the top, and he was once again studying the mechanism that ran the clock and worked the pendulum.

Pepper and I reached him a few moments later.

'I think this proves that the stone circle is our girl's prison. Don't you?' Martin said.

'But what good does that do us if she tears those stones up?' I said.

'There's only one thing we can do,' Martin replied. 'Destroy the clock and the pendulum. But something about the workings just doesn't add up. I'm trying to figure it out.'

'Show us,' I asked. 'What's wrong with it?'

'You see the cogs?' Martin said.

I nodded.

'They don't turn consistently. It's all random, as though this thing is working against itself. It's not like any clockwork I've ever seen before.'

I looked closer, and sure enough, the cogs and wheels turned at opposing angles. When you really studied it, the whole thing was impossible.

'What does it mean?' Pepper said. 'I feel like I'm looking at hieroglyphics or something.'

'You're right!' exclaimed Martin. 'It's a language!'

'How can cogs be a language?' I said. It didn't make sense.

'We've been looking at this all wrong,' Martin said. 'These *aren't* cogs we are seeing. It's a spell. Written on the wall.'

As Martin said this, I did stop seeing cogs and began to see pictures instead.

'How?' I asked.

'The important thing now is that we stop the clock working and the pendulum swinging,' said Martin.

As if to underline the importance of this, the tower shook again.

'Break the spell?' I said.

Martin nodded. 'I have to understand it before I can

do that though.'

He began to study the words, running his fingers over them as though that would help him fathom their meaning.

'What is that? Some kind of red paint?' Pepper asked.

'Blood,' said Martin. 'And there! It looks like a strand of hair weaved into the wall.'

I looked at the hair. It was the same colour as Isobel's. But it was long, as long as the fairytale character Rapunzel's, and I could see how it worked its way like vine leaf over and through the wall and the cog-shaped words.

'It's holding the pendulum!' I said in a moment of epiphany.

'I think you're right,' Martin said. He scraped at the hair with his fingers, and the strands cut into him, sharp as a razor. Blood tarnished the hair, and the cog words began to move again.

'Yes, oil it,' came a voice behind us.

With all of the movement of the tower I had been unaware of the arrival of Vincenzio. He now stood on the platform behind us.

'I had to oil it. Before you came,' said Vincenzio. 'But then she loved you more than me.' His face was distorted with rage and insane jealousy.

'You oiled the cogs with blood?' Martin said.

'It gives her energy,' Vincenzio said. 'Only I can do it. It's my right.'

He dived at Martin, but Pepper struck him hard on the back of the neck, felling him before he could vent his anger.

'He's lost his mind,' Martin said.

'She was still controlling him,' I said. 'Is he going to be all right?'

Pepper kneeled down and checked him. 'He's just unconscious. I'm certain he'll be fine when he wakes – if we can finish this and stop Isobel from getting free.'

Martin returned to his study of the hair and cogs. Then he shook his head. 'The only way is to break the strands – but look where that got me.' He held up his hand, and I could see fine paper cuts on his fingers.

I had stowed my knife back into my boot as we had climbed the steps, and now I removed it and held it out to Martin. 'Try this.'

A banshee cry echoed up from below, and a huge tremor sent the three of us toppling. The knife fell from my hand and skidded across the platform. I pulled myself up and dived for it. The knife skittered over the edge, but my fingers caught it just before it could fall.

I turned back to see the Xana now on the platform beside us. She had finally broken through the restraint of the stone circle, and here she was, ready to regain her full power.

She was beautiful again – radiant, and in Isobel's form – and I saw her hypnotic power reach out to Martin and Pepper. I stumbled back to my feet and rushed to my two friends, only to have Pepper turn and point his gun in my direction. I halted.

'You're too late,' said Isobel, and now her hair was growing long and extravagant, penetrating into the walls as her strength grew.

What the devil was she?

She was like nothing I had ever seen before, and I felt her power reaching out to me also. If I waited any longer I might not be able to stop her.

I tried to look Pepper in the eyes, but found his attention on Isobel: it gave me the time I needed.

I leapt up, tumbled past Pepper and fell forward,

slicing with my dagger at the hair that was growing into the wall.

Isobel screamed. Blood leaked out of the walls and dripped down over the spell, running into the cogs; but this time it didn't feed them. The hair had been severed from its source of power. The spell on the wall smeared and blurred.

Isobel fell to her knees as Pepper turned back toward me, levelling the gun directly at my face.

He was going to kill me. Even now, she had full control of him.

'Pepper!' I pleaded. 'Don't let her control you.'

He cocked the gun.

'I don't blame you. It's not your fault. But I have to tell you I love you, Pepper, and I can't hide it anymore.'

Pepper blinked. His finger twitched on the trigger, and then his arm dropped down.

The Xana sobbed at my feet.

I looked down at her and saw a young girl, with hair now cropped off at her shoulders.

'I was so vain about my hair,' she said now. 'My father built the tower, and then a demon came. He took possession of it. Killed my father. Then he used me to feed his magic. I was the bait for thousands of men that he murdered and fed on. I wasn't born a Xana, I was an ordinary girl.'

'Where is this demon now?' asked Martin.

'As I grew in strength he began to fear me. Then he trapped me in the stone circle and left. I have no idea who he was or where he went.'

I wondered if she was telling the truth this time, and decided to believe her, for now. She was too weak for guile, and all of the evil I had sensed in her appeared to be gone.

We helped the Xana and Vincenzio, who was coming round, up onto their feet and down the wooden staircase.

At the front arch of the cave we found Beth and Brewster. Both appeared well but confused. They had no memory of their captivity, and neither did Vincenzio.

While we had been gone, Carlos had braved the cave-that-had-been-a-house and retrieved our luggage. The trunks were now stowed onto the back of the carriage.

Pepper led Vincenzio, Beth and Brewster to the carriage, then he and Martin came to the cave opening where I stood with the Xana.

'What are we going to do with her?' I said.

'Her power and her own imprisonment are ended,' said Martin. 'We should let her go. Hope that she doesn't try to join with evil again.'

'Are you sure that's a good idea?' Pepper wondered. 'I mean. we don't know for certain that she's okay.'

A mighty crash of tumbling rock, solid stone and brick drew our attention back in the direction of the tower.

My colleagues and I hurried around the large rock formation and discovered that the tower had completely collapsed. Behind the rock, the former garden and stone circle lay in ruins. I knew then that any remaining source of power was completely gone.

I glanced at the Xana. She was no threat: just a lost and lonely girl, barely older than 16 or 17. What harm could she do now? And more importantly, where could she go? She had been under a spell for centuries. There was no family for her to return to. The sad truth was that she had been a victim in all of this.

I sent my cat senses out, seeking for any sign of a glamour or power that might be confusing and beguiling us still. There was nothing. It appeared that this was, finally, the truth of the situation.

'Come on,' I said taking her arm. 'Let's get out of here.'

# Epilogue

As we drove away from the rock and its myriad caves, the desert sand gave way to a path and then a road. We turned toward a vineyard, and there, just beyond several acres of land, lay a house. A mock castle. A folly. It turned out it was the real home of *Don Vincenzio*.

'Beth and I were travelling home from our honeymoon,' recalled Vincenzio, 'and we met Dr Brewster along the way. He had come to greet us.'

'Yes,' agreed Beth. 'And I saw the rock and caves, and asked if we could stop and explore.'

'It was then she took possession of the three of us,' Brewster added. 'We've been under her control for months.'

'But what about Nicolas?' I said suddenly. 'Was he real? And the others I saw dancing?'

'No,' said Martin. 'I believe he, like the cook and the other servant, Matthias, were changelings. She created them when they were needed, but didn't have the strength to keep them all there at once. It's why we never saw any other servants. And those dancers were merely phantoms used to keep everyone there.'

Carlos pulled the carriage up in front of a large door fronted by a set of stone steps.

There was no courtyard, or wall, but otherwise the castle was similar to the illusion the Xana had created. I was soon to learn, though, that the dungeon was one of a number of embellishments that had made the drama of the whole castle work better as the Xana drew on its captives' imaginations.

Around the large dining-room table in the spacious reception room we ate real food for the first time in days.

'I guess she created the castle from my memories,' Vincenzio said. 'It's ridiculous that we were so near and yet so far from our real home.'

'And now what are we going to do with you?' Beth said, looking at the Xana. She smiled at the girl. Her eyes were kind: she was so like Martin.

'You all saved me,' she said. A shy and sweet girl whose memory of the events and the years of her slavery would slowly become more dreamlike every day.

'I guess you'll just have to become our ward,' said Vincenzio.

'Really?' she said. Her eyes shone with hope for the first time since we had left the caves.

'But you are banned from ever returning to the rock,' said Martin.

The girl smiled at him, and Martin blushed and looked away. Perhaps he had some residual feelings for her. I made no comment. Instead I glanced at Pepper. He was looking back at me.

Things had definitely changed between us, and this

was no spell. That was the one thing in this world I was certain of.

Under the table I reached for his hand and squeezed his fingers.

I was still wearing the ring.

# About the Author

Award-winning author Sam Stone began her professional writing career in 2007, when her first novel won the Silver Award for Best Novel in the *ForeWord Magazine* Book of the Year Awards. Since then she has gone on to write several novels and novellas and many short stories. She was the first woman in 31 years to win the British Fantasy Society Award for Best Novel. She also won the award for Best Short Fiction in the same year, 2011.

Stone loves all types of fiction and enjoys mixing horror (her first passion) with a variety of different genres including science fiction, fantasy and steampunk.

Her works can be found in paperback, audio and e-book.

# More Titles By Sam Stone

### <u>KAT LIGHTFOOT SERIES</u>
Steampunk, horror, adventure series
1: ZOMBIES AT TIFFANY'S
2: KAT ON A HOT TIN AIRSHIP
3: WHAT'S DEAD PUSSYKAT
4: KAT OF GREEN TENTACLES
5: KAT AND THE PENDULUM

### <u>JINX CHRONICLES</u>
Hi-tech science fiction fantasy trilogy
1: JINX TOWN
2: JINX MAGIC
3: JINX BOUND (Coming 2017)

### <u>THE VAMPIRE GENE SERIES</u>
Horror, fantasy time-travel thrillers
1: KILLING KISS
2: FUTILE FLAME
3: DEMON DANCE
4: HATEFUL HEART
5: SILENT SAND
6: JADED JEWEL

THE DARKNESS WITHIN: FINAL CUT
Science fiction horror short novel

ZOMBIES IN NEW YORK
AND OTHER BLOODY JOTTINGS
Thirteen stories of horror and passion and six mythological and
erotic poems from the pen of the new Queen of Vampire fiction.

POSING FOR PICASSO
A supernatural thriller (Coming 2017)

www.ingramcontent.com/pod-product-compliance
Lightning Source LLC
Chambersburg PA
CBHW060752210726
48292CB00014B/2768